Tender Mercies

Jessie Gussman

Published by Jessie Gussman, 2022.

TENDER MERCIES

First edition. July 8, 2022.

Written by Jessie Gussman.

Cover art by Julia Gussman[1]
Editing by Heather Hayden[2]
Narration by Jay Dyess[3]
Author Services by CE Author Assistant[4]

LISTEN TO THE INCREDIBLE Jay Dyess bring this book to life on YouTube HERE[5]. Listen to more than thirty professionally produced Dyess/Gussman audios for free on SaywithJay!

CLICK HERE[6] if you'd like to subscribe to my newsletter and find out why people say, "Jessie's is the only newsletter I open and read" and "You make my day brighter. Love, love, love reading your newsletters. I don't know where you find time to write books. You are so busy living life. A true blessing." and "I know from now on that I can't be drinking my morning coffee while reading your newsletter – I laughed so hard I sprayed it out all over the table!"

---

1. https://sweetlibertydesigns.com/services/

2. https://hhaydeneditor.com/

3. https://www.youtube.com/c/SaywithJay/

4. http://www.ceauthorassistant.com/

5. https://youtu.be/zKOfrcBY0Qk

6. https://BookHip.com/FASFD

Chapter 1

Iva May clenched her hands in front of her and walked to her kitchen door. She'd asked Bev and Bill to meet her in her kitchen in her home not far from the church in Blueberry Beach after the Christmas Eve service.

Bev was already there.

Bill had just arrived. He stayed longer after the service to make sure everyone got out okay and to help clean up afterward.

Iva May took a deep breath, closing her eyes, then blowing out slowly.

It didn't really help with the nerves that made her whole body feel like she was on fire despite the tiredness she fought.

She'd kept a secret for forty years, but tonight it was going to come out.

She had to let it out.

Pressing a hand on her stomach, she thought about her recent doctor's visit and the cancer that had spread through her body. If she didn't divulge the secret now, she might take it to the grave with her, and...while that was tempting, it wasn't right.

It hadn't been right to keep it to begin with. To do what she had done.

"Iva May?" Bev's voice held concern, and rightfully so maybe, since she'd stopped halfway to the door and just stood there with her eyes closed and her hand pressed to her stomach.

She took another breath, blowing it out before turning with what she hoped was a reassuring smile toward Bev.

"I'm fine," she said, knowing it was mostly true. She would be fine. Hopefully would be fine.

She hadn't wanted to lose Bev's friendship. She hadn't wanted to hurt the good man that Bill had become. And, if she were being honest, she hadn't wanted to lose her reputation in town.

That had gotten more and more important as the years went by.

All of it had.

A lie never got easier to correct.

Another soft knock at the door spurred her feet, and she moved the rest of the way, opening the door and smiling at Bill. His forehead was wrinkled, his brows drawn, his eyes concerned.

That was Bill, always worrying about other people, putting himself last, if necessary.

Last to leave the church, last to be served, last to reap any benefits, but the first to give.

Even if she were ten years older than he was, they'd still made a good team through the years.

He had money to give, but he hadn't wanted to be the face of it. Hadn't wanted to have the whole town knowing that he was behind a lot of the good works that happened in Blueberry Beach. Saving the train shop. Supporting the new consignment store in town. A generous donation to the ice-cream shop, and paying unexpected bills and in general doing whatever he could for the businesses along the main street in Blueberry Beach.

It had all been Bill but coordinated by Iva May.

"Are you okay?" he asked, apparently being able to immediately read the uncertainty in her eyes. Or maybe the nervousness. Or maybe her fear was leaking out.

Before she could answer, his eyes seemed to be drawn to the table, and his focus went there. Iva May stood close enough to him that she could feel the shock that went through his body as his eyes met Bev's.

Guilt pinched the fear away.

Had she caused their breakup?

She had. She knew she had, but at the time, it seemed like the right thing to do. She hadn't done anything with the intent to hurt them.

She hoped they believed her tonight.

"If you wouldn't mind sitting down?" she said to Bill, who still stared at Bev, his face hard, expressionless, although she could feel the slight tremble in his arm when she touched it, turning him toward the table.

If this was how he felt forty years later, she should have stepped in, instead of keeping the secret and making it even worse with her actions.

Bill gave her another glance, then put his hand over her fingers on his arm, patting them, like he knew she needed the reassurance.

She definitely did.

She blew out another breath. This was why she hadn't tried to do this before. She knew it was going to be one of the hardest things she'd ever done.

Bill put a hand on the chair, but he made no move to sit down.

Bev no longer looked at him but slowly stirred her tea, the spoon clanking against the glass, loud in the otherwise silent room.

"Can I get you something to drink?" Iva May asked Bill.

He shook his head.

"Please sit down." Maybe her face held pleading, or maybe his legs were shaking as much as hers were. Whatever it was, he gave her one glance, then pulled the chair out from the table and sank into it slowly, his hands resting on the table, not folded, just...lying there. Ready.

Ready to strangle me.

"I had wanted to do this when my daughter, when Kim, was here, but she couldn't make it," she began, her hand on the back of the chair. Now she was the one having trouble sitting down.

She turned to the refrigerator, opening the door and pulling out a cold bottle of water. She set it on the table in front of Bill's place.

It was winter, Christmas Eve, and cold water probably wasn't what he wanted to drink, but she needed something to do with her hands.

Something to do, period.

"Does she need a ride?" Bill asked, immediately concerned.

"No. She has her car back, but...she just couldn't make it."

Iva May tried to keep her worry from showing on her face. She was going to be dumping enough news on them. They didn't need to know that she suspected Kim had cancer. After all, she'd been at the doctor's multiple times, and she seemed to go back monthly. She'd recently split from her husband, and her daughter who had been going to start college decided to move to LA and become an actress instead.

It felt like Kim's life had been falling apart all fall. Iva May loved her daughter with all her heart and had been slowly falling apart inside as well.

Maybe Bill was responding to the tension in the room, as he seemed to deliberately relax his hands. But, as though he couldn't quite make himself be still, he slowly spun the water bottle in front of him, the plastic label crinkling as he did so.

Iva May tried to channel some of the peace from the recent Christmas Eve service into her soul.

Christ had come so that she could be forgiven.

Christ had loved and forgiven.

Christians were supposed to love and forgive.

If only that were true. Sometimes it seemed like Christians were the least forgiving, least loving people on the planet.

But not Bev and Bill.

She had to believe. Believe that they would hear and understand why she had done what she did, and forgive. Love her anyway.

Sitting down in her chair, she touched the handle of her coffee cup with one finger while trying to figure out where to start.

With her cancer diagnosis? No. She might not even tell them that.

With Kim? No. She wanted to build up to that.

"I guess you guys are wondering what I might have to tell you?" She looked between the two of them, Bill's eyes concerned, worried, his whole being looking like he was ready to sweep her off her feet and carry her away to somewhere safe.

He was like a son, and the idea made her smile. Someone who loved her so much, he'd want to protect her with his life.

Her eyes shifted to Bev, a true friend. There might be a decade and a half between them, but that made the relationship almost like mother and daughter. She wished it were true.

Love shone from her eyes, but there was speculation there too. Bev was more intuitive than Bill, and Iva May knew she already suspected tonight was going to change her life forever.

Chapter 2

Bev met Iva May's eyes, concerned. Iva May had been acting strangely all evening. Particularly since she told Bill and Bev that she wanted them to come to her house after the service.

She refused to tell them why, even though Bev asked. It was odd for Iva May to hide anything and refuse to answer a question.

When Iva May had told her she wanted to meet after the service, she hadn't mentioned Bill. Had she been afraid Bev would refuse? Bev wouldn't have told Iva May no, even if that meant she'd be around Bill.

But Bev had been beside Iva May when they met Bill just inside the church, and Iva May had issued her invitation to him. Bev had barely been able to concentrate on the sermon.

Even though the Christmas Eve service was her favorite service of the year.

How could she?

Not only did Iva May know she avoided Bill at all costs and yet had somehow decided that it was a good idea for both of them to be in her house after church, but Bev squirmed at the idea of being that close to Bill. It had made concentration almost impossible.

She'd ended up in a loveless marriage with a man who cheated on her, thankfully having an ironclad prenup that enabled her to keep everything she'd built.

But after that... After all hope of having any semblance of a family had been taken from her, she found it harder and harder to concentrate on business, and she spent more and more time in Blueberry Beach, until she'd almost semiretired and wasn't needed much at all at her corporate office in Detroit.

"We were in the hospital together when our babies were born." Iva May's voice cut through her thoughts, and Bev looked up.

Iva May had acted like she was going to say something Bev didn't know.

But she knew that.

She dropped her hand from her spoon and stared at Iva May, nodding when Iva May seemed to be waiting for some kind of reaction

"The nurses told you your baby died."

Iva May's words somehow seemed fatalistic, and when she said "your," she looked to both Bill and Bev as though making sure that they knew she knew they were the parents.

Bev nodded slowly. That wasn't common knowledge in town. She had only been fifteen, and at the time, the age of consent in Michigan had been seventeen. Her parents could have prosecuted Bill. He could have been sent to prison.

In Bill's defense, he hadn't known how old she was, because he'd believed her when she lied to him.

"And our babies were in the hospital nursery at the same time."

Somehow that struck her like...like there was something big about to happen in her life.

Iva May took a deep breath.

"Let me start at the beginning." Her voice sounded shaky, like she was scared.

Bev kept her eyes on Iva May, even though she was very aware of Bill sitting to her left at the round table. Patience seemed to settle on him like a blanket. If he was tense, she couldn't tell. She didn't look at him but was still hyper attuned to every move he made.

How could she not be? Despite the attraction that had always been between them, an attraction she wished she could ignore, he was a good man. Steady. Dependable. Kind. Considerate, honest, and loyal. She could go on.

Iva May did go on about him when they were alone in her house. Almost as though Iva May had to convince Bev that Bill was single and available.

Bev didn't need to be convinced. But she had been in one bad marriage; she wasn't going to make a second mistake. And, as good as Bill was, men changed after they married a woman, taking her for granted, ignoring her, acting like she was dumb and a pain to boot.

Bev had seen it over and over again in her friends' marriages. She'd experienced it in her own.

She had absolutely no desire to tie herself down to a jerk again.

No matter how attractive Bill was. No matter how many memories there were between them.

"I had extremely bad anxiety after I had my baby. I don't know if it was because of my age or what, but I couldn't stay in bed. I felt the need to go somewhere, anywhere, but of course I couldn't leave the hospital."

Iva May had begun to talk, and it was almost like she couldn't stop. She didn't pause even to take a breath.

"They wouldn't let me keep my baby with me in the room, so I walked the halls, watching the nurses as they cared for the little ones, and...I heard some things I might have been better off not knowing."

Her lips had flattened, and she looked down.

"That's not true. It's not that I would have been better off not knowing. It's that I would have been better off because I would have made different decisions, I think."

She said the last two words like she really wasn't sure even now if she had done the right thing.

Bev held her breath.

"I heard Darla."

Bev tried to keep her gasp silent, but she wasn't quite able to smother it. Her eyes flew to Bill.

Darla was the woman Bill had cheated on her with. Everyone in town knew Bill and Darla were together after Darla had announced it to everyone who would listen.

No one in town knew about Bill and Bev.

Bev needed to see Bill's reaction. Did he still look guilty all these years later? Not even a little. She couldn't believe the calmness in him. He didn't even look upset.

It made her mad.

But she bit her tongue, unwilling to interrupt Iva May just to give the man a piece of her mind.

She'd been clear forty years ago.

"I hadn't been able to sleep all night, and I went outside early that morning, just walking to try to relieve my anxiety, and I didn't understand at first why Bill was even in the parking lot of the hospital. But I heard Darla tell you she was lying about you," Iva May said, her voice soft and almost compassionate as she looked at Bill. "I heard her say that she would quit lying if you would do what she wanted you to."

Bill's finger moved just a little, as though he were acknowledging that was actually what Darla had said.

"Somehow she knew you had money. A lot of it. And she was basically blackmailing you. Telling you she would let everyone know she had been lying about you guys hooking up, if you would pay her."

Bill nodded, his gaze thoughtful as though he were remembering.

"You agreed to pay."

Bill kept nodding.

"But she never kept her word," Iva May stated flatly, and Bill gave one last nod and then looked away. "And you shoved a bag you'd been holding at me and asked me to give it to Bev. I didn't understand why in the world you'd want to give something to Bev, but I took the bag and you left."

Bev's mouth had opened. Shock and surprise raged through her. Had she seriously believed a lie all these years?

"I could have told you the truth." Iva May's gaze was now directed at her, and Bev, still reeling from the fact that Bill hadn't cheated on her all those years ago, narrowed her eyes at Iva May. Why had she kept that a secret?

"But there's something else." Iva May's tone again took a fatalistic turn. And Bev closed her mouth. What else could there be?

Beside her, Bill tensed as well. Whatever it was, he was bracing himself for the shock.

She couldn't look at him though, didn't want to see the disappointment on his face. See that for all these years she'd believed Darla, even though Bill had proclaimed his innocence.

He'd never mentioned his money. That had been new too.

"I don't know if you remember," Iva May said, looking at Bev. "But that small hospital had been very busy that evening. They only had four rooms, and all four of them were full. I had my baby a day before yours, and then you'd had yours, and then two more women had come in."

"I remember. I can still hear the screams when I close my eyes."

"Yes. Exactly. They were both having a hard time, and the staff was overworked and unused to so many babies in such a short time."

Bev remembered. One of the nurses had told her when she was discharged that the last time they'd had four babies at one time had been ten years previous, nine months after the worst snowstorm of the century.

At the time, Bev had chuckled, thinking about the unintended consequences of being snowed in.

Now...she hung on Iva May's next words.

Chapter 3

"They called in a nurse who had very little experience, and somehow she managed to get our babies confused. I only knew this because she had been explaining it to a coworker over the coffee break, when I happened to be walking by after being outside with Bill. It interested me, obviously, since I was sure I would be able to tell which one was my baby."

She took a deep breath. Then she went on.

"I went in to check on them in the nursery. The two nurses were on break, and the two other nurses were still dealing with the mothers in labor. I... I felt like I could tell which baby was mine. But the one I thought was mine was in the bassinet with your name on it." She looked at Bev. "It was blue."

Bev looked down. She fiddled with the handle of her tea. She hadn't taken a sip since she'd sat down. And no wonder.

"I swear. I swear on all that's holy, I never touched the babies. I didn't. But I'm sure as a mother could be that nurse mixed them up, and my baby was the one who died."

Bev couldn't move. She searched in her memory for some idea that she'd had any inkling that the baby she'd been handed and told had died during the night hadn't been hers. She hadn't known. Hadn't suspected. Had looked at the child and never thought it didn't look like the newborn that she'd delivered, only cold and stiff and very, very dead.

She swallowed, but her throat was dry, and she ended up coughing instead.

Bill had stood from his chair, leaning over the table, his hand going toward her, like somehow her coughing was more serious than what it was.

She put a hand up. She didn't want him to touch her.

Couldn't stand it.

Not after everything she'd found out tonight.

"Did you ever have Kim tested?"

Bill's voice cut through the tension in the kitchen. Or emotion. It was a feeling in the air so thick she felt like she could reach out and touch it.

Iva May shook her head. "At first, I couldn't stand the idea of losing her. And while I was almost certain I was right, there was a chance that my intuition was wrong, and I was making a big deal out of nothing. I'd overheard a random comment from a nurse saying she had trouble telling the babies apart, and the one in your bassinet had died. I thought maybe it was survivor's guilt, or a variation of that, where I couldn't stand the idea that you'd lost your baby and I didn't, so I transferred what I remembered of my baby onto yours. I don't know." Her breath trembled out, and she slowly shook her head again. "I had so many things I wanted to do, and yet a mother's love for her child is so strong, and my desire to have a baby—all those years of infertility and now I had my miracle child, and could I really have her take a test that could take her away from me?"

She lifted pleading eyes to Bill, who, while he didn't exactly look compassionate, nodded, seeming to understand.

"You were in a stable marriage. And you'd seen me in the hall with Darla."

"If anything, seeing what I had with Darla made me think that if you were the father, you'd be a good one. My..." Her eyes slid to Bev's, and she seemed apologetic, remorseful. "You were only fifteen."

Bev was already nodding. She needed to process. Had never considered that it wasn't her baby that died. That there might be a woman walking the earth who was her child. Had been her child over the last forty years and she hadn't even known.

It made her sad and angry and frustrated, but she had to be honest.

"I don't know how many times I've told you over the years as we've sat right here in your kitchen that it probably was a good thing my baby died. Not that it made me happy," she was quick to add. "But because I was only fifteen."

She couldn't help it. Her gaze slid to Bill's. She'd told him she was eighteen. She'd said she was a year behind in school. All lies.

When she heard about Darla and Bill, she'd told him the truth, and to her shame, she'd taunted him with threats of calling the cops and reporting him, pushing for a conviction. She almost went as far as to claim that she hadn't been a willing participant.

She hadn't been able to get those words out of her mouth, because it had been the exact opposite. She'd been the one to convince Bill what they'd done was a good idea. Because, even though he believed that she was eighteen, he'd wanted to be married first.

It had been an argument between them. But the kind of argument that didn't include anger. Just something they didn't agree on.

Bill had sat back down, and while there wasn't any expression on his face, it wasn't hard to see the pain in his pinched skin and tense knuckles as he gripped his water. She'd hurt him then. And he'd never stopped hurting.

Funny how humans gave some people that power over them. The power to hurt.

Bill had given that power to her. She'd known it at the time and had sworn she'd never use it.

After all, when someone loved another person, they were vulnerable. They trusted. They gave their word. And they opened themselves up to the potential for a lot of hurt.

She might have only been fifteen, but she had vowed that she would never hurt the man who had finally relented and become her secret boyfriend.

And yet...she had.

In her defense, she'd only done it because he'd hurt her first.

Except... He hadn't. She'd just believed the rumors.

"So you're telling us that Kim might be ours?" Bill's voice was hesitant, but deep and laced with something that sounded an awful lot like...disbelief, mixed with excitement.

It was kind of how she felt, only there was a lot of guilt mixed in.

"Why did you never tell me about Darla before this?" she asked Iva May. Maybe she should have waited until they were alone. After all, she didn't really want to discuss it in front of Bill. Because...he had done everything right. Other than being intimate with a woman that he wasn't married to, and that had taken a lot of convincing on her part.

Although that was part of the reason he hadn't wanted to date her while she was still in school. He hadn't wanted to be tempted, and he hadn't wanted to get married before she graduated.

She almost closed her eyes and looked away, but she focused on Iva May as Iva May chose her words carefully.

"You just said you told me over and over how even though you were devastated that your baby died, you knew that the Lord worked that out for your good. That you wouldn't have developed the business that you have, and you wouldn't have been successful. Not with a baby, and...not with Bill."

Iva May's last words were slow as her eyes skittered to Bill.

Bev wanted to shrink into her chair, because it was true. She had often said she would have loved her baby no matter what, but she wouldn't have been successful in business if God hadn't taken her. And she also said that had she married the baby's father, she probably would have ended up staying in Blueberry Beach, being a mother and housewife. She wouldn't have been anything else all of her life.

Honestly, she wasn't sure that was a bad thing. After all, after the heartbreak of her marriage, she'd been left alone, with nothing but the hollow comfort of a successful business and wealth beyond her wildest dreams—empty victories without someone to share that success and wealth with.

She wasn't sure she wouldn't trade a lifetime romance, and a good man who loved her, for all the money and prestige she had.

"It's true. I wouldn't be a successful businesswoman. I wouldn't be a millionaire. I wouldn't be any of the things I've turned out to be." She spoke to Iva May, and she noticed out of her peripheral vision that Bill didn't move.

She couldn't tell him that she regretted her decisions.

That would be admitting that she was wrong.

That would be admitting that she wanted him.

That would mean...she still loved him.

If there was one thing that her marriage had taught her, it was that she couldn't be vulnerable.

Especially with Bill, because he owed her. He'd been vulnerable with her, and she hurt him. Badly.

He would most definitely want to get her back. Men were like that. Competitive. They cared about the score. Her ex always got her back worse and more any time he perceived a slight on her end.

It was just the way men were.

"You never gave my bag to Bev?" Bill asked, as though that were important.

"No. I wish I had it to give her now, but...after her baby died, I threw it away. It honestly wasn't until weeks later that I realized you must have been in the parking lot that early because you were the father, and after I thought about that, I realized that the age difference between the two of you was probably the reason you were there so early—so no one would see you two together."

"I take it Kim doesn't know?"

Iva May shook her head, meeting Bill's gaze, even though her finger still fidgeted. "She doesn't suspect a thing. And...actually, I suspect there's something wrong with her. I know she's been to the doctor's. More than once. It seemed like a regular thing, and...the only thing I can figure is cancer." Bev gasped, but Iva May said quickly, "I'm just speculating. I don't know anything for sure."

"She should be tested. I have the breast cancer gene." Bev glanced over at Bill, thinking at the last moment that admitting this in front of him might not be a good idea, but Iva May prompted her, "Go on?"

Bev deliberately turned from Bill and lowered her voice. "I had a double mastectomy fifteen years ago. I carry the gene, and it just seemed like a good idea. If Kim hasn't been tested, she should. She's...the same age as I was when I had my operation."

Bill's hands wrapped around his water bottle, the knuckles white.

She wasn't sure what that meant, but she wasn't going to look at his face. She didn't want to see his disgust. Or relief. Relief that he wasn't married to someone who would do something so drastic to something that made her female.

It had been a hard decision. A tough one for her to recover from.

Her husband at the time had not been supportive. In fact, they'd had a big argument about it. He didn't want to be married to a woman with no breasts.

She had wanted to be dead.

But she hadn't wanted to die. If that made sense.

In her mind, she had bigger concerns, but convincing Richard of that had been impossible.

Eventually she'd had the surgery without his consent.

Maybe that had made it even harder to recover from. The idea that she was no longer appealing in her husband's eyes.

Not that keeping her slender figure had kept him faithful at any point in their marriage. She just hadn't wanted to be a statistic. Another divorce. Maybe she hadn't wanted to be alone, either, since children were out of the question. Richard hadn't wanted her. And she couldn't imagine anyone looking at her and seeing anything worth wanting. So she stayed.

Until he had left her.

Apparently one of his girlfriends insisted on marriage.

The idea still shot sadness through her, and anger as well. Since she'd worked so hard to stay, and he'd walked away so easily. It didn't seem fair.

"There's something else," Bill stated flatly, looking at Iva May.

Whatever he thought about the idea that they could have a child together, about their old relationship, about the fact that she admitted that she was wrong, wrong about so many things, none of it was showing on his face.

Just concern. An inquiry.

What else could there possibly be? She looked at Iva May and knew immediately that Bill was right. Funny, because Richard would never have thought to check. He wouldn't have noticed.

Bill was different.

But he was still a man. And regardless of how perfect he was, she didn't want to be trapped in marriage again.

Shoving those thoughts aside, she reached over and put a hand over top of Iva May's, which was fisted on the table.

"Something more to do with us?" she asked, not sure she could take any more information today. It was Christmas Eve and supposed to be a happy time. She felt like she'd just been struck with a hundred-pound weight.

"No. This is my own personal battle."

"And we're your friends. You share your personal battles with your friends." Bill had taken her other hand, and they sat there at the table, each of them holding one of Iva May's hands.

This woman who had just completely changed their lives and determined a new direction for them, this woman who'd been like a mother to her, a good friend, a benevolent member of the community. She held an explosive secret, several, now she had something else.

"If it's something that you don't want us to tell anyone, we can keep it to ourselves," Bill said, looking over and lifting his brows, prompting Bev to squeeze Iva May's hand.

"You know we're good for it," she said reassuringly. Funny how she could sound so calm when her entire being was swirling. Swirling with the ideas planted in her brain this evening.

But Iva May's problem was more pressing.

"Can we help?" she asked gently.

Iva May smiled sadly and shook her head. "I wasn't going to tell anyone. Not until after the holidays. I... I didn't want to depress anyone or attach sad memories to this holiday which is supposed to be nothing but happy."

"But there's something. Now that we know there is, you're going to tell us," Bill said firmly, not giving her room to back out.

Iva May looked up, her blue eyes sad, her brow wrinkled. "I decided to tell you about Kim tonight, not because I have character. Not because the guilt was consuming me. But because...I was diagnosed with cancer this past week. It's all through me. Inoperable, and no point in treating. It's...just a matter of time."

"No!" Bev said, reeling back, her hand slipping from Iva May's and both of them going to her chest. Iva May was a rock. She couldn't have cancer. People like Iva May didn't die. They lived forever dispensing wisdom and smiles and cookies and laughter and warm places that felt like home. They weren't like other people.

Iva May could not die.

But she was nodding her head. "I have a meeting with hospice the day after Christmas."

The fact that she'd been wrong about Bill, the fact that her baby might not have died, that she might have a daughter alive and walking the earth, and that she'd done a good man wrong—they had all been terrible truths that she needed to adjust to and internalize somehow, but the idea that Iva May might die?

This was by far the worst.

"How long did they give you?" Bill asked, his voice more caring and concerned, more gentle and compassionate, and just hearing it made Bev want to cry.

"They said three to six months. I think it's not going to be that long."

Bev couldn't handle it anymore. She had never broken down in front of her husband, she had never broken down because of her husband. She didn't cry in front of people, but this was more than she could take.

She stood from her chair, knowing Iva May was in good hands with Bill sitting beside her, and rushed out the door before they saw the tears streaming down her face.

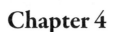

Chapter 4

Bill forced himself to stay seated and did not follow Bev out the door like he wanted to.

His whole body wanted to move after her, comfort her, work this out together.

He always had that urge when Bev was around. Whatever was going on, he wanted to share it with her. How much more, news like this?

His hand tightened on the old fingers in front of him, and he looked into Iva May's face. Her eyes had followed Bev out the door, sadness etched in every feature. Dark, like the lake on a cloudy day.

"I knew this was going to be a lot for someone to take in," she said, almost as though she were talking to herself. "I wasn't going to mention my cancer."

"I'm glad you did, and I'm sure Bev is too. We want to know, even if it is a shock. We love you. I can't even think about Blueberry Beach without you. We've done so much together over the years. You've influenced so many."

Her eyes, sad and tired, moved to his, and her lips trembled a little as they tilted up. "That's kind of you to say."

"I mean it. I think Bev could handle everything else, but the idea of losing you... It's too hard."

Iva May was quiet for a moment. Her face, though still tired, held thoughtfulness and almost a plea. "I was hoping... I hoped telling you two together would... Well, I've never been a very good matchmaker. And I'm sorry."

Her words were disjointed, thoughts left open-ended, ideas not finished. There was so much in her expression, but words just didn't seem adequate.

"You don't need to apologize. The Lord works everything out for a reason. It would be arrogant of me and disrespectful to God to lay blame at your feet for the way my life turned out."

"Bev deserves a man like you." Iva May spoke softly.

Bill shook his head. "I've never amounted to anything. Not by anyone's standards. My marriage was a failure. Fatherhood was a failure, since my girls don't even talk to me. I inherited a fortune, and yet all I've done with my life is to be a shop owner in a sleepy little town."

How true. No one would look at him in any way and say he was successful. Let alone someone like Bev. Someone beautiful and classy and who had built her business from the ground up, almost single-handedly. She would never *deserve* a man like him.

Maybe she would *settle* for him.

But that was his dream. Not hers.

"I don't think that this diagnosis has given me a new perspective, because I always knew I was going to die. But if it makes more sense to think about it that way, go ahead, because this dying woman says the kind of success you're talking about doesn't matter. And when I say she deserves a man like you, I'm talking about your character and the solid, honest man you are. Not your success according to the world's terms."

Iva May could always get to the heart of the matter. He always admired and eagerly listened to her wisdom and advice.

She might be dying, but this was one time he couldn't listen to her.

"My character is iffy. The very fact that I might have a child I never knew about attests to that."

"And if everyone were judged on what they did when they were twenty, none of us would have any character."

That might not be entirely true, but hopefully it was accurate to say that he wasn't the same man today he was forty years ago.

"Bill?" Iva May asked as though they weren't in the middle of a conversation.

It made him think that whatever she was going to say was something important to her. He put his second hand over top of the one of hers he already held and closed it in his calloused fingers, giving the cold, wrinkled skin some warmth.

"Yeah?"

"I have a favor to ask of you." Her eyes glittered a little, and the smallest smile spread on her lips. "You wouldn't deny a dying woman her last request?"

He appreciated Iva May's humor. Appreciated that she didn't take life so seriously that she couldn't smile, even in the face of death. It made it easier for him to handle. To know that she wasn't upset about it. Or at least, if she were upset, she could still laugh about it.

"Of course not. Whatever you want me to do, I'll do it." He didn't usually make promises lightly. Especially one this big. But he trusted Iva May. She wasn't going to ask him to do anything impossible. She was going to ask him to do something that was good for her and probably even better for him.

"Court Bev. Marry her. Spend the rest of your life with her."

His mouth opened. He closed it, but it opened on its own again. Once more he closed it.

His head wanted to shake. An automatic "no."

"I can't promise to marry someone. That involves two people's decisions. Not just me."

"If you are vulnerable to her, if you let her know you love her, that you love her no matter what she does to you, that you want her no matter what happens, that you think she's amazing no matter what she does, that you admire her, respect her, and will be there for her... No woman can resist that. And Bev already loves you."

Be vulnerable?

Tell Bev his feelings without any guarantee that she would reciprocate?

Be in her life, even though she didn't want him? Open himself up for ridicule and rejection?

Wait. Iva May thought Bev loved him?

Iva May didn't say anything while he grappled with all his questions and his dawning astonishment. She didn't need to remind him that he'd already promised that he'd do whatever she asked.

He swallowed, because he'd much rather she asked him to build the Taj Mahal or swim across Lake Michigan in the winter. Or take a fork and spoon and dig a grave in the frozen Michigan ground.

Any of those things would be easier than what she asked.

Even if Bev really did love him, which he just couldn't believe. Iva May wasn't often wrong, but she was definitely wrong about this.

Bill always kept his feelings close, hiding them with a veneer that was part sarcasm, part intelligence, part sage wisdom.

Most people didn't know how he really felt.

It felt dangerous to even think of sharing that with anyone.

"I'll do my best," he finally said, although it was unnecessary. He'd already promised.

Iva May nodded.

He wanted to hug her and moved to get out of his seat. But he could tell from the look on her face that she had something more to say. So he sat still and waited.

"I know I just gave you a lot of information that was a shock to you. And you seem to be handling it well, even being strong for me. Which I appreciate." She lowered her head a little, acknowledging the strength he was lending her. "But I've had several days to get used to this diagnosis, and I'm at peace. I didn't choose to be born, and I don't get to choose when I die."

That was the kind of wisdom that Iva May had about God that he wanted to just bottle and drink as an elixir, making him wise.

He nodded.

"Right now, I am fine. But..." She tilted her head, pleading with him to understand. "Bev is not. Please. If you can. Find her. It's Christmas Eve. She's alone. She's scared and upset, and she won't want to cry on my shoulder now. She won't want to upset me. She'll want to be strong for me. So, she needs you. Please?" Iva May said it simply, like it was the most natural thing in the world for him to find someone that he wasn't even sure liked him. Whom he had a not-happy history with. Whom he still felt attraction for, even if she seemed cold and distant and like she'd rather be anywhere than with him.

"If that's what you want? Are you sure you're okay if I leave?" It seemed like when he knew someone was dying, he couldn't just get up and walk away from them, leaving them alone. It was like an unwritten rule of the universe.

"When a woman is dying, you can hardly deny her request. You never know when it's going to be her last." Iva May's eyes had a little of the old twinkle in them as she spoke. Teasing him some, and he couldn't help but smile, although his face felt heavy like a beach towel full of sand slung over a fence, dripping down.

"I'm not crossing Jordan alone," Iva May said, easily reading the sadness on his face.

"That seems like one of the hardest things we do in life, and we all have to do it alone. Without our human friends anyway."

"I guess that's a good reason to be good friends with Jesus."

"Then I guess I'll leave you here with Jesus, and I'll go find Bev. If I can." He wanted to anyway. Even if she didn't want him, he always wanted to be where she was.

"The church. That's where I'd go. Or she might have gone home. There isn't really anywhere else. Unless she's standing on the beach, although that would be cold."

Those were the three places Bill had already thought she might be.

But he didn't say that to Iva May. She would probably just smile and act like that meant that they were meant to be together, when he was pretty sure that it didn't mean any such thing.

So he simply said, "Thank you," and rose.

He paused, still feeling bad for walking away.

"Go on. I promise you can take care of me later, but Bev needs you far more than I do right now."

Bev had always struck him, even as a teenager, as the kind of person who didn't need anyone.

Maybe that was part of what was so appealing about her. She always seemed to know what she wanted, and she knew how to get it or would work until she figured out how.

And that included him.

She'd lied about her age in order for them to be together, because he flat-out refused to date someone still in high school.

He took one last glance at Iva May, who waved him away, before he settled his beanie hat back on his head, grabbed his coat, and walked out the door.

He wondered over the years how he could have been so stupid. Mistaking a fifteen-year-old for an eighteen-year-old. Believing her when she said how old she was.

But he found, as he lived his life, people had a tendency to believe what they wanted to believe. And he definitely wanted to believe she was old enough.

He also found that five years didn't usually make a huge difference.

Although, the five years between a fifteen-year-old and a twenty-year-old were a lot bigger spread than the five years between fifty-five and sixty years old.

Shoving his hands in his pockets, he debated about walking toward the church or toward Bev's house.

But neither one of those places was the place that he would be. And while he and Bev were different, especially when people looked at their personalities, he thought, particularly back in the short time they'd been together, that they were a lot more alike than what they seemed on the surface.

So he turned, without thinking about it again, and headed toward the beach.

Chapter 5

B ev stood beside the water as the wind gusted, cold and hard, blowing across her cheeks, filling up her hood, whipping her heavy wool skirt around her legs, and making her wish she were anywhere else.

Who was she fooling? It wasn't the wind that made her wish she were anywhere else.

It was Iva May and babies and cancer and...Bill.

He seemed so strong. Hardly any reaction to the words that spilled out of Iva May's mouth. Words Bev didn't want to hear. Words painting pictures she didn't want to see.

She didn't want to think she'd missed her daughter's entire life.

She didn't want to think she'd made a mistake when she believed Darla.

She didn't want to imagine she'd left a beautiful life here in Blueberry Beach and lived one that, the more she thought about it, the more it seemed like it was wasted.

But, most of all, she couldn't imagine the woman who had been like a mother to her all her life had not only been keeping this shocking secret from her the entire time but was now dying of cancer.

How could she be so angry and love someone so much it hurt all at the same time?

How could she be fifty-five years old and still feel attraction for the first boy she ever loved?

Maybe he was the only boy she ever loved.

But he was sixty now, and so different. Still, the promise of character and integrity and humble service to others had been there early in his life. All she had to do was listen to her conscience to believe that.

Even the mistakes he made as a twenty-year-old hadn't taken away from the promise of the man he'd become.

She was the one who had always pushed for more. He'd been the one to say they should wait. But she hadn't wanted to, and he hadn't understood. Not why she didn't want to tell anyone about their relationship, and not why the idea of waiting was so difficult. She knew it was going to be another three years before she graduated.

He had not.

She hadn't even begun to process the idea that together they might still have a child, a daughter. That their baby hadn't died. Over the years, she considered that, multiple times, it had been a good thing. Always with a grateful heart, not that their baby had died, but knowing that because she had passed away, Bev had been able to do all the things she'd done.

Her life would have been much different if God hadn't taken her baby.

Apparently He hadn't.

She wiped the tears from her face. Tears she hadn't even thought about shedding. They just seemed to come.

She wasn't a crier. She never cried. Not in front of people, and not even in private. Very seldom.

"Iva May wanted me to find you. Make sure you were okay."

That voice came out of the darkness. Deep and strong and so very welcome, she felt she could lose herself in it, filling her until she didn't know where it stopped and she began.

That was whimsical thinking, thinking she didn't engage in. She was a practical businesswoman, analytical and driven. She didn't waste time on daydreams and impractical thoughts about voices and losing herself in them.

"We can go back and tell her." Her voice was cool, her head still facing the lake. She didn't turn to him, although she didn't figure he could see the tears on her cheeks, even if she had.

Even if he saw them, he most likely wouldn't ask about them.

"Christmas Eve on the beach sounds like a good thing for Floridians, not Michiganders."

"There was a year, back when we were together, where it was seventy degrees on Christmas Eve, and we spent the whole day on the beach," she said softly, not even sure why. She didn't want to relive memories with this man. She wanted to cut him out of her life and never see him again. He was too tempting. Too much what she'd always wanted and never had. Too much what she knew she should have gone after, instead of wasting her life the way she had.

Bev snorted at that idea. Most people would not say building a multimillion-dollar business was wasting her life.

This man beside her, being with him was exactly what she should have done. Any second spent without him had been wasted.

That was foolish, schoolgirl-dream thinking. The kind of thinking she didn't allow herself.

"I remember that. One of the best days of my life."

She swallowed, her throat feeling dry and harsh. "Mine too."

She didn't want to relive old memories. Didn't want to feel any more connection to Bill than she already did. But she couldn't seem to stop. Like she needed his strength. In some manner, he'd been able to tell. He'd been able to find her. Who would expect someone to go stand out on the beach when it was twenty degrees outside with the wind whipping off the water making it feel even colder?

"Our daughter could still be alive," she said. This didn't upset her nearly as much as Iva May's cancer, maybe that's why she couldn't talk about it.

"That was a shock." Bill paused. "Is that why you're out here? You're angry?"

"No. I can't be upset about it. I mean—" She stopped. She didn't want to tell him that she felt like maybe her life would have been better off if she would have spent it with him, so instead she said words that were just as true. "Iva May made a better mother than I ever would have. I couldn't have chosen someone I would rather have had. So... The idea that I missed out on my daughter's entire life is hard, but I can't help but feel that Kim has become a better person because of that."

"Stop. That's not true. You are an amazing person, and you were back then as well."

She snorted derisively. "You don't even know me."

"I've heard about you from Iva May. Not just about your success in business, which is impressive, of course."

She didn't think Bill was any more impressed with her success in business than she was.

"But about your compassion. About your generosity. The way you help people, and the things that you've done outside of your business." He'd been facing her, but he crossed his arms over his chest and turned, standing shoulder to shoulder with her, looking out on the deep darkness of Lake Michigan. "She's proud of you. Like a mother."

"I love her like a mother." The words were absolutely true, and Bev had to swallow the lump of grief that threatened to choke her. She couldn't imagine life without Iva May. "I want her to get a second opinion."

There. She'd broached the subject that was the hardest.

"I think she should too. But if the cancer is all through her, it's not like there is anything that can be done."

"I know. I just want her to do something. Take treatments. Do anything that might keep her with us longer."

"Make her miserable in the process?"

"I know. I'm being selfish. See? I told you that you don't know me."

"Everything you just said I want too, because I don't want to lose her any more than you do."

"But you're not selfish enough to say or insist on it."

"Neither are you." His words were spoken with confidence, meaning that she wasn't going to insist that Iva May needed to take treatments that were only going to make her miserable, and he was right.

"You're right. It's her choice. I just... I just don't know if I want to be here to watch her go. But I know I need to be. She deserves to have people around her who love her and not have me abandon her in her time of need."

A gust of strong wind blew, cold and harsh, and Bev wrapped her arms around her stomach over her coat.

Bill stepped closer. His hand settled on her shoulder, heavy and somehow comforting through her layers. "No one is going to abandon her. Least of all us. What she said tonight was shocking for me. I assume it had to be just as much so for you. But I know it didn't change a thing about what I think about Iva May or how I feel about her."

Bev didn't have to think about it. "It didn't change anything for me either."

"You're handling everything else really well." His words were said almost as a question. Like he was asking her if she was handling everything as well as she seemed to be.

"You can't see my tears."

That seemed to take him off guard. Like he hadn't been thinking that she would cry. She didn't know what made her say it, anyway, since tears were something she'd always hidden, and she didn't want to share the most vulnerable part of herself with this man, no matter how much character he had.

"You're too strong for tears," he said, something that sounded like wonder in his voice. She figured she had been right—he didn't think she cried.

Normally she didn't.

"I told you, you don't know me."

"I've always wanted to."

The breeze took his words, whipping them about in the cold darkness, wrapping them around her, twining like ribbons, wanting to warm her with their unexpected surprise. They settled deep in her chest, maybe not the most welcome words she'd ever heard, because she didn't want to go there with Bill. Their relationship was long past, and if they got together now, it would make her regret the choices she'd made in her life.

Not that she didn't already have regrets.

Deciding her best option was just to pretend she didn't hear what he said, she spoke. "We're going to need to take care of Iva May. I'm sure hospice will be great, but they're not twenty-four-seven care. She'll need us."

"And she'll have us. It's not going to be a hardship to close my shop. I'm never busy in the winter anyway. I've already thought of that and don't have a problem with it."

She should have known he was already on it. For herself, she had some loose ends to tie up in Detroit in order for her to be here without interruption. But they were loose ends that she'd been neglecting for a while.

"I've been planning to move to Blueberry Beach permanently for over a year. I will have some things I have to take care of, but I can work those around whatever schedule we need to set up for Iva May."

"We'll need to talk to Kim when she comes." He paused. "Have you heard anything about her?"

"Just what Iva May said to us. That she thought she might have cancer too. We might not be able to count on much help from her if that's the case. In fact, she might need us. She might...be ours." That thought was so foreign. So unexpected. She couldn't help the next words that she said. "Do you think she looks like us?"

"I've always felt an affinity toward her, and as I was sitting in the kitchen with Iva May, and she said what she did, I realized it was because she looks so much like you. My affinity isn't in a wrong way, just I've always wanted to help Iva May with her, and I have."

"I wasn't even here." She didn't want to be bitter about it. God's hand was on her life, and He had been in charge, allowing it to work out the way it had.

"Iva May was an excellent mother."

"I know. Better than I ever would have been." She did feel bitter about that. About the fact that he had hinted that Kim was better off with Iva May.

"I didn't mean that the way you just took it. I didn't mean that Iva May was better than you. I meant that what you've done with your life so far—because it's not over yet—was a good thing, and Kim did not suffer because you weren't with her. She had a good mom. Although she would have had a good mom if you had her."

"She would have had the best dad."

"I wouldn't be so sure about that. My ex and my daughters don't agree."

Chapter 6

Bev gasped. She'd known Bill was married and had thought she heard rumors about children, but she hadn't been back at all for several years, and she completely missed meeting any of them. It hadn't been hard to forget because she hadn't wanted to remember. Nor think about the idea of Bill with anyone else.

"I can't imagine. Even at twenty, you were an amazing man. There is no way you could have gotten married and not been an ideal husband and father."

She didn't want to get back together with Bill. She really didn't, but she wouldn't allow him to think less of himself than what he was.

"My ex would disagree with you. My daughters would too."

Suddenly she was curious. Why? How? What had he done? What kind of person was he? Did she really not know him?

"I've seen you for years through Iva May's eyes. She's pretty much told me everything I know about you. And that never includes a single bad word. Ever."

"Iva May's opinion is biased. She likes me."

"You're the father of her daughter."

He was silent as though digesting that information. "I never thought about that. You're right. Maybe I felt so comfortable with her because she went out of her way to make sure I did. To make sure I was around as she was raising Kim."

"Same. She always made me feel welcome." Then Bev shook her head. Suddenly she was cold. "She is hospitable to everyone. That's how she makes everyone feel."

"Come on. You're cold. Let's at least walk to my shop. Or I can drive you home."

35

"My house isn't far. Especially if I just walk up the beach. Half a mile. I walked to church tonight."

She needed the time to think. Needed time to process another Christmas and the fact that her life hadn't turned out the way she wanted it to. That there was something wrong with her because her husband wouldn't stay. Wasn't happy with just her.

"I'll walk you there."

He didn't wait for her answer but took ahold of her elbow through her coat and gently turned her until they were walking side by side.

"I guess everyone knows everything about everyone's lives in Blueberry Beach."

"I can't be with Iva May and not know all there is to know about you. Or at least all she knows. You're her favorite subject," he said as they walked along through the darkness, the waves crashing along the shore, making soothing sounds but still somehow showing the power contained within. Just something about the rhythm, the rhythm of nature, slow and steady and unceasing. Everything underlaid with the hand of God holding it all together. That was the part that was probably the most comforting to her. Knowing that God's hand was everywhere. Keeping the waves on the shore. Keeping the water in the place He created for it.

She hadn't stayed in her place.

She could have been beside this man for the last forty years.

No regrets. She whispered those words to herself before she pushed all of those thoughts out of her head.

"When I'm with Iva May, her favorite subject seems to be you."

Bill just grunted as they walked a little further on the beach in silence, his hand still on her elbow. Not pushing her, not even guiding her. Just there. There to let her know that if she needed him, he was there.

It was the kind of comfort she craved. The kind that didn't overpower her, the kind that didn't ignore her, the kind that didn't find someone else better or something else he'd rather be doing. Just letting her know he was right where he wanted to be—beside her.

"I wasn't going to tell you this, but tonight, while I was sitting at the table after you left, Iva May told me that her last request from me was..." His voice trailed off, and Bev tilted her head, looking over at him. Wondering what in the world would Iva May have asked him to do.

"For us to take care of her? For us to take care of Kim?" She hadn't even processed Kim, but there was no way she wasn't going to be as involved in Kim's life as Kim would allow. Not that she hadn't been involved before. Kim was probably the second person that she texted the most after Iva May.

"She wanted..." Again, he paused.

It was so unlike him to be so indecisive she almost stopped.

But she was cold and eager to get home. Maybe eager to see Bill's face in the light.

She wouldn't invite him in. She didn't want to get any closer to him than she already was. Although, if they were coordinating Iva May's care, she would be working with him for...months? Iva May could defy doctors' expectations and live for years. She truly hoped so. Even if that meant she'd be spending more and more time with Bill.

"If it's hard for you to say, you don't have to tell me." She wasn't sure where those words came from, because they weren't what she wanted to say. She wanted to demand that he spit the request out immediately. "This is something that involves me too? Is she going to ask me the next time she sees me?"

"I don't know. I... When we were saying that when I'm with her, she talks about you, and when you're with her, she talks about me, maybe she'll do this too. But... Basically she wanted us to get together. She wanted me to see to it. I told her that it takes two. It's not just me."

Bev stopped, the sand soft beneath her feet. She sank in and twisted toward the man beside her. Although she wasn't sure why she was looking at Bill. She wanted to be anywhere but beside him.

"This is...awkward," she said, although she didn't mean that. Not really. It wasn't awkward, it was exciting. The deepest desire of her heart. And Iva May had to know it.

Had Iva May told Bill that just because Iva May wanted to give Bev this one last thing?

Or did Iva May know it was what Bill wanted too?

That Bill could want her was hard to believe. That Iva May could know it was even harder, but it was so hard to tell with Iva May.

"Yeah. I didn't say it to Iva May, but I don't want to be with someone because they're fulfilling the last request of a dying woman."

"There are worse things to build a marriage on," she said, turning and starting out again. His hand came back to cradling her elbow. Just there. Not pushing, not controlling, just being there.

Would that be what marriage to Bill was like? Someone to walk beside her. Someone devoted to just her.

As she would be to him.

Not someone controlling her when he wasn't ignoring her.

"I guess we could pretend until..."

"Yeah. I guess we could. But Iva May's a pretty astute woman. Not to mention, I'm not good at deception."

She loved that about him. Loved his honesty. Loved that if he wouldn't lie to an old woman even to make her happy in her dying days, he wouldn't lie to his wife.

"What made you and your wife split?" She didn't need to ask that, and it wasn't exactly what she wanted to know anyway. "Why does she say you're not a good husband? And your kids? Why do they think you're not a good dad?"

Didn't they know how rare honesty was? How rare it was to have someone who actually spoke the truth. Said what they really felt and didn't deceive, not even with little "white" lies, which were probably more harmful than anything else. Because they allowed a person to believe that they were doing good, when God clearly despised all forms of deception.

The lights at her house were almost directly to the right, and she started to turn.

Bill turned with her, and she remembered how she wasn't going to ask him to come in.

But she was curious enough about his wife and children that the invitation was out before she even thought about it. "It's Christmas Eve, and I hate to send you back down the beach without some hot chocolate. Do you want to come in for a bit and tell me about it?"

He seemed stiff beside her. Where before he had been completely relaxed, at least until they started talking about Iva May's request.

"It's boring stuff and not necessarily stuff I'm proud of."

"I don't want to force you to do anything, but you're welcome to come in."

"I guess I'm wondering how we went from talking about how I don't want to deceive Iva May to you asking about my ex-wife."

"Because. I love that you don't want to lie. I love that you don't even want to twist things to make them look like something that they're not. I love that, and I think it's rare. And it makes me wonder how your wife couldn't have seen the value in that about you. Because I remember clearly back when we dated, you hated the fact that I wanted to hide our relationship. It wasn't just because you were proud of me. It was because you didn't want to deceive people. Honesty is a beautiful thing in a person."

Maybe she said more than she should have. Maybe she didn't want him to know how much she admired that, and him.

But then again, maybe she did. That was being honest. And while she had worked extremely hard to get where she was with her business, she had never been dishonest. She had met an awful lot of dishonest people, far more dishonest people than people she trusted.

Bill was one of those—people she trusted.

"You don't have to stay if you don't want to. It's not going to hurt my feelings, but... I'd like you to."

Maybe she just didn't want to have to think about all the things that Iva May had confessed, or maybe she was looking forward to the opportunity of discussing them with him and getting his take, because there would be no one else in the world who would understand like him.

"Okay. I'm not staying long."

Chapter 7

Bill walked into Bev's house, feeling out of place. It wasn't fancy, exactly, but it felt rich and bright, and he didn't even have words to describe what the stuff was he was standing on in her kitchen. He just knew it was shiny and looked like it had cost a lot of money. High ceilings, big windows, and white everywhere, with art that probably cost more per piece than his surf shop made in a year.

He hated feeling so out of place, but he'd never been in Bev's house, and he looked around with curiosity, wanting to understand this woman that was so much a part of his life, so much a part of his thoughts.

"Don't worry about taking your shoes off," she said as she slipped her boots off and slid her feet into slippers that were sitting by the door.

"No. If that's what you do, that's what I'll do."

"You're not staying long. And it doesn't hurt anything. Just cuts down on the amount of time I have to spend cleaning."

"You don't have someone clean for you?" It looked like the type of house that would take a whole army of people to clean, and Bev seemed like the type of woman that would have them.

"No. Cleaning is actually therapeutic for me. I get a lot of thinking done, and it's satisfying to see things sparkle when I'm finished."

He thought of the dingy surf shop. Cleanliness was not his first priority. That would be having things on hand his customers wanted. Things that would make their vacation more enjoyable. Things that they could afford and that would give them hours of family fun. That was his priority.

He hadn't even thought about the dirt in his shop until she mentioned about liking things to sparkle. He swept the floor every day but didn't think about anything...sparkling.

It probably looked poor and dingy to her. The same way her house looked rich and beautiful to him.

"When Iva May talks about you, she always says Bill said this and Bill said that. And I always have such a hard time imagining it, because Bill doesn't say much of anything to me." She looked at him from under her lashes, raising her brows, as though she were offering him the floor in case he wanted to defend himself.

He set a second boot beside the first one and straightened. "Maybe Bill just likes looking at you, and words seem to ruin everything anyway."

Her lips flattened, like his answer did not please her, and she jerked her head toward the kitchen island.

"You can sit there while I get some milk warmed up. Unless you'd like something else?"

"Hot chocolate is fine." It wasn't his favorite, but if that was what she was drinking, he wasn't going to ask for anything special. It was just enough to be at her house, watch her graceful movements, see her long slender fingers and the swish of her hair as she worked to serve him. Not that he got a great kick out of people serving him, he just admired Bev no matter what she was doing.

"You were going to tell me about your wife and daughters," she said, standing in front of the refrigerator door with her hand on the handle, questions in her eyes.

He shrugged out of his coat and set it over the stool beside him, deliberately not meeting her gaze. Thinking.

He'd always felt that he made a mistake in marrying Mardi. He'd felt that way at the time. And over the years, the feeling hadn't dissipated, until about a decade ago. And then, maybe he just had a lot of growth in his life, or maybe he'd finally been old enough to reflect a little more honestly.

Or maybe it was something Iva May had said, but his eyes had been opened and he realized that their poor marriage and divorce hadn't been all her fault. He'd been just as much to blame. Maybe more.

Bev poured milk into a pan on the stove, and he smiled. He would have expected her to use the microwave, since she didn't seem like an old-fashioned kind of person. But she turned the stove on low and then turned around, facing him with her arms crossed, her eyes curious. Questioning.

"I shouldn't have married her."

There. That was the truth. And that's why everything was his fault.

"Someone forced you into it?" she asked, totally misunderstanding him.

"No. It'd been ten years after you and I...went our separate ways."

They could hardly break up since they weren't officially together to begin with.

She moved her head just slightly, acknowledging his words.

"It took me about that long to figure out you were never coming back." He swallowed and looked down, but didn't want to appear weak, so he forced himself to look back up, meeting her gaze. "I started to hear rumors that you were becoming successful. I knew you weren't going to leave that success and come back to Blueberry Beach. Up until then, I had hoped that something would happen."

"Did you hear I was married?"

"I did. But half of all marriages end in divorce. I wasn't hoping for the destruction of your marriage, not really, but that could have been something that would have sent you back home."

Her lips flattened again, as though she wanted to disagree. And she probably would be right in her disagreement. Even if something had happened to her marriage, she wouldn't have come back home. Bill could see that now. She wasn't the kind of person who did anything with her tail between her legs.

She grabbed life with both hands and wrestled it into submission, making it what she wanted out of it.

"So, when Mardi showed interest in me, I convinced myself that I liked her too. And before I knew it, we were married with a child on the way."

"Before you knew it?" she asked, almost as though she didn't believe him.

He nodded. "I couldn't have you. So I settled. I shouldn't have. It was a mistake and a disservice to Mardi. She deserved a man who loved her the way I...should have."

Maybe Bev knew that he almost said *the way I loved you*. If she suspected it, she didn't say anything. Just turned to the stove, pulling a spoon out of the drawer and stirring the milk.

"That doesn't explain what the problem was. Plenty of marriages survive, even thrive, without there being a huge amount of romantic love, just good solid friendship."

"There wasn't even that. She was so far away from my type, it wasn't even funny."

"Your type? You have to have a type in order to get along?"

His type was Bev. Whatever Bev was. Strong and determined, in control yet vulnerable, and compassionate. He could see the thickness of her lashes and the moisture that still clung to them, where she'd been crying. He knew she had that vulnerable part, and it made him want to protect her, even knowing she didn't need him, since her *allowing* his protection would almost be better than her *needing* it. It would say she *wanted* it. Even though she could handle things on her own. Like opening up a little secret door and letting him into her life versus him barging through and forcing his way in.

"No. She just hated it here in the small town. Hated my shop. Hated the hours I worked. My shop doesn't make enough for me to hire someone, so in the summer, I work a lot. She wanted to travel. Wanted to go to Europe. Wanted to take the girls when they got older."

"How old were they?" Bev asked, shaking the spoon and setting it aside, then looking at him over her shoulder.

"Kelsey was three, and Anna was just one when she left me. But she talked about Europe, and I couldn't have been less interested. She talked about traveling in the States, and I wasn't interested in that either."

"You've always been a homebody."

"Mostly. Although my roots are in the UP."

"You can say that if you want to, but you are more connected to Blueberry Beach than some of the people who were born and bred here."

She got it. She didn't seem the slightest bit surprised that he wanted to be home. Didn't want to travel. And she knew how much he loved Blueberry Beach.

He didn't want that to affect him, but it did. Maybe she'd spent more time getting to know him than what she wanted to admit.

"None of that explains why she would say, or why you would believe, that you are a terrible husband and father." She leaned against the counter, and once again, her arms were crossed over her chest, almost as though she were challenging him.

He couldn't help it. He grinned at her. Loving that she seemed to be defending him. He had other people who had defended him, other people who believed in him, people who told him that it wasn't his fault, that Mardi was impossible to please, but having Bev believe in him? It was better than having the rest of the world at his back.

It always felt like if he just had her by his side, they could face anything together.

She hadn't agreed.

"She got angry and bitter. Rightfully so. I didn't even consider traveling with her. I could have." He had the money. The money he'd made from selling his property in the UP to developers. But he'd always used that money for others. It wasn't money he wanted for himself. He supposed, looking back, he should have been more considerate of what Mardi wanted, even if it wasn't anything he was the slightest bit interested in.

"She accused me of not spending time with her. She was right. She accused me of working too much, not making time for family." That had hurt. He'd always made time for his daughters. "But I couldn't afford to hire someone at the store, and she thought anything more than an eight-hour day was too much." He sighed. "I could have done all the things she wanted me to do."

"Did she do what she wanted? Did she take your wants into consideration?" Bev hadn't moved, but her face was hard. She was angry at Mardi.

He almost smiled, but guilt kept him from it. "No. She wanted me to do all the changing, but really, I was happy with her the way she was. She wasn't perfect. No one is, and when she moved into a separate bedroom shortly after she got pregnant with Anna, it was completely understandable. She said I snored, which I do."

"That's just part of being married. Putting up with people's faults."

"I have a lot of faults."

"Maybe you weren't the only one who wasn't completely invested in the relationship," Bev said, before her eyes widened, and she looked back at the stove. Just in time as the milk had begun to simmer, and it started climbing up the sides of the pot.

She shut the stove off and grabbed a spoon, stirring it and moving it off the burner.

She let it sit there while she opened the cupboard and pulled out the chocolate mix.

"You might be right. I was a rebound relationship for her." In fact, she had told him that the man who had broken up with her before they got together had been the love of her life. She made no bones about the fact that she would never love anyone the way she loved him.

He'd heard rumors over the years that they'd had an on-again, off-again relationship after she left him. Maybe they had, he didn't know. And he hadn't cared enough to check it out. Which probably said everything that needed to be said about his dedication to Mardi. Especially since it had been a relief when she left. Except, his heart had gone with his daughters. What was left of it, anyway.

"So she was just angry and bitter?"

"No. I told you. She was right in all of her accusations. I hadn't spent time with her, I hadn't given her what she needed. I hadn't been completely invested in the relationship." He thought he was being a good husband. And he knew he had been the best father he could be.

"What about the girls? You said they said you were a terrible father?"

"They don't talk to me."

"What happened?"

He shifted in his chair. This was the part of his story with Mardi that really hurt.

"She moved to North Carolina. Obviously we couldn't trade weekends, and while I considered selling the surf shop and moving closer to her, ultimately I decided not to. They came up for four or six weeks in the summer. Of course, that was my busiest time, but... I always thought they had a good time with me. Still, every year they grew more and more distant, and... I think Mardi poisoned them against me, or maybe I just really don't know how to be a dad. Because, surely they would see my actions, and if Mardi were lying, they would know it. By the time they hit their early teens, they said they didn't want to come anymore, and they were old enough to make that decision. I haven't talked to either one of them in over ten years."

"You've made an effort?"

"I just mailed them Christmas cards last week. I always do. Last year, Kelsey's card came back "address unknown." And when I called Mardi and asked for her new address, Mardi told me that maybe I should have been a better father, and she would have given it to me herself."

"That's harsh." Bev's face scrunched up before she turned back, stirring chocolate into the cups.

"There. Does that satisfy your curiosity?"

One side of her mouth pulled back, almost as though she wanted to say that it didn't.

"I still have questions, but I appreciate you telling me as much as you did. I feel like you were a good husband, although you could have been better. But...is anyone perfect?"

He thought that himself. He couldn't blame his incompetence on his age, since he'd been thirty when he got married. But he'd been self-centered. Maybe a little annoyed that the woman he married wasn't more like Bev. Or maybe he was just annoyed because the woman he married wasn't happy with him the way he was and wanted him to be different. Maybe they were both wishing that the person they married was more like the person who didn't want them to begin with.

"No. You're right. Still, for years I blamed her. Since I'd put all of my effort into the marriage. The only thing I didn't do was travel, because we couldn't afford it. Unless I dipped into the money I had set aside to help others. And I would have done that, for my girls, after all, I always spent that money on helping others, but Mardi left before we could even think about a European trip, and I just always assumed that her biggest beef with me was that I wasn't her ex."

He paused for a moment, and then he said honestly, as honest as he could be, "Since that was my biggest beef with her."

Bev picked up a coffee mug in each hand and turned toward the bar, setting a mug down in front of him. "That makes me sad. It hurts too. But I suppose there's also a part of me that...likes? Maybe that's the word I want. Likes that you held my memory up as a gold standard that couldn't be met." She smiled sadly. "We both know I'm definitely not a gold standard." She shook her head as she spoke.

"We don't both know that. In fact, I disagree."

He wasn't going to let her believe a lie. She might have only been fifteen, but she made a mark on him that lasted a lifetime.

"Maybe you're just one of those men who fall in love one time and never fall in love again."

"Maybe. Sometimes I wonder if I even have feelings. After all, I long for my girls and wish I had a relationship with them, and I would do anything I could for them even if they came back tomorrow, not apologizing, just needing something from me. But... I don't think I have feelings."

Not since Bev had left. It's like he'd sealed himself off and hadn't allowed himself to get close to anyone or anything, other than maybe Iva May.

Everyone else, he just sat back and looked at, dispensing wisdom, offering benevolence, showing compassion, covering everything with a hefty dose of sarcasm, but never love. He didn't want to open himself back up to that kind of pain and grief and hurt.

Interesting, since somehow, he hadn't even realized it, but Iva May had seen that about him, had touched on the one thing that he needed to do, that he wouldn't do. And that was to allow himself to feel again.

Chapter 8

Bill knocked on Iva May's door at nine o'clock on Christmas morning.

He'd already made plans to be here, and what he had learned last night hadn't made him change his mind. In fact, he was eager, especially since Kim's car was parked in the driveway.

Mostly eager. There were some nerves that made his stomach clench.

Not enough that he wished he'd taken up any of the other offers he'd had from the residents of Blueberry Beach to spend Christmas with them.

His neighbors had invited him, since this was going to be their first Christmas without their grandfather and grandmother. Both of whom had passed away this past fall.

And now Iva May. So much death.

Death was just part of living and not necessarily something to be dreaded, since rather than an ending, it was more truthfully a beginning. The beginning of a soul's eternity.

But still, there was loneliness and heartbreak from the ones who were left behind.

Bill didn't necessarily think that his work on earth was finished.

Iva May's impending death made him think about his own mortality which he didn't want to do because he wasn't ready to die. He had so many things he wanted to accomplish. For a surf shop owner with no ambition, he had a lot of people he wanted to help, and maybe, maybe part of it was also the fact that in his heart of hearts, he hoped that the relationship with his daughters could be patched up.

Even though it had been decades. Still, he hadn't lost the hope that he held close to his chest—that his daughters would eventually see him for...not a perfect man but someone who loved them and cared for them. Someone who had been shut out of their lives, not because he wanted to be, but because he hadn't had a choice.

Maybe he should have fought harder for them. That was the doubt that often went through his head.

He didn't wait for the door to be answered, but rapped on it, and then walked in. Even as he was stepping in, he could hear Iva May calling from the living room, "Come on in!"

He put the fruit salad he carried on the counter on his way through the kitchen, shifting the bag of gifts he brought into his other hand and walking into the living room.

He could tell as soon as he stepped in that Iva May had told Kim what she told them last night.

Kim looked at him with apprehension, like she was worried he might have some kind of negative reaction.

How could he? Kim might not have been the successful businesswoman Bev was, but she was a good person. Kind and generous, sweet and helpful. She wasn't selfish or rude, and while she could have spent more time with Iva May over the years since she'd left, he understood why she didn't.

She had not been married to a good man, and he demanded a lot from her.

"Merry Christmas," he said to the room in general, including both Iva May and Kim in his words.

"Merry Christmas," they said back to him.

Iva May opened her mouth to speak, with a crease in her brow, and he smiled at her reassuringly.

"It looks to me like you told Kim what you told Bev and me last night."

The worry smoothed out of her forehead immediately, and she smiled. The tiniest bit of apprehension made it tremble. "I did."

"And I said that I couldn't think of better parents, even though I love Iva May and always will."

Kim's words warmed Bill's heart. He hadn't considered that she might not want him to be her father. But the thought hit him that she could have had a very negative reaction, or even denial, to Iva May's confession.

"I don't see any need for a paternity test, unless you're going to insist upon it." She paused delicately. "I can understand why you might want one."

"I don't. I don't want to disrupt anything you have with Iva May and your late father. Not trying to step in or step on anyone's toes. But I'm happy to be as much of a father as you want me to be."

The last line was kind of hard to say, because he'd been rejected as a father by his wife and daughters. It made him feel like he wasn't good enough. That there was something wrong with him that would keep him from being a good dad. The insecurity was there, planted and watered by years of being rejected at every turn. No matter what he had done, no matter what he had tried, they hadn't wanted to have anything to do with him, although they never rejected his money.

That was a completely different story.

Kim's smile was a little strained. "It might be a little early for me to even think along those lines. I'm still adjusting to the fact that Mom might not be my mom." She waved her coffee mug carefully in the air. "With the idea that she wasn't truly sure that she was my mom all these years and never told me." She lifted her eyes on that last bit, giving her mom a reproving glance.

That was when Bill realized that Iva May hadn't told her the rest of her news.

The cancer news.

"But I guess you were always there for me growing up. Did you suspect?"

Bill shook his head automatically. Kim was a good bit older than his own daughters, but because of his relationship with Iva May, and the benevolent things they did together, and also because Kim was the same age as the daughter he and Bev had lost, he always had a special affinity for her.

Her recent divorce had been hard on everyone, not necessarily because Kim loved her husband so much, but because she had fought so long and so hard to stay in her marriage, and her husband had only been interested in himself, and what benefited him, and hadn't hesitated to ditch Kim as soon as someone with money came along.

"Where's Alyssa?" he asked, referring to Kim's daughter.

Kim's face fell, and he regretted his words. Obviously wherever she was, it was hard for Kim. Particularly since today was Christmas.

"She told me she wanted to spend Christmas with one of her roommates, but it's kind of ironic that that roommate is from the same town as her dad's new wife."

There was some bitterness in Kim's voice, and Bill couldn't say he blamed her. He understood exactly how it felt to lose your child to someone who you didn't feel deserved her.

"I'm sorry. Are you seeing her later?"

Kim shook her head. "She was spending the holidays with them."

Her lips pressed together, and all semblance of a smile had fled.

Bill wanted to put his arm around her and comfort her as a father would his daughter, but his relationship with Kim had never been touchy-feely. In fact, he didn't have a touchy-feely relationship with anyone.

Except Bev.

As though his thought had conjured her up, there was a knock on the door, and then Bev called out, "Hello?"

Iva May spoke loudly. "Come on in! It's open!"

The nerves that had been absent as he thought about meeting Kim, and all the things that might happen as Iva May told her secret, erupted in his chest. Which pinched painfully.

He and Bev had parted on good terms the night before, but she'd been clear about not wanting him. And he felt like a fool, because he'd told her so much, given her so many details that he never shared with anyone, and she hadn't realized how special she was to him. Treating his confessions like common information and treating him like a distant acquaintance.

It shouldn't bother him, and mostly it didn't; it just felt painful. Like one more rejection.

He straightened as Iva May said, "I didn't offer you any coffee." He noticed then that her voice sounded much more tired. Maybe because she'd been trying to hide her lack of energy from Kim.

"Don't worry about it. I know where the pot is, and... Bev, would you like coffee?" he asked as Bev walked in the living room.

"Sure. I'll take a cup."

"Black?"

She blinked, as though she were surprised he remembered that was the way she had taken it all those years ago.

She recovered quickly though, he'd give her that, and nodded her head briskly. "Yes, please."

While in the kitchen, he could hear some murmuring and wished he wouldn't have chosen that moment to leave the room. He wanted to know what Kim was saying to Bev. Was Kim more interested in a second mother than she was in having a father at all?

He supposed that didn't really bother him, because it would probably make Bev happy, and anything that made Bev happy made him happy too.

He poured the coffees, noticing the two pumpkin pies and some kind of covered casserole sitting on the table.

Bev hadn't been much of a cook back when they dated. In fact, he wasn't sure she could even make boxed mac and cheese.

It kind of surprised him that she could cook or bake at all now, considering her success in business. He would have thought it wouldn't have given her time to learn.

Although Bev was nothing if not determined. If she wanted to learn to cook, she would.

He carried the coffees back in the room. They kept talking as he listened.

"I wasn't thinking a DNA test was necessary, either. I've always loved you, and while I've never thought of you as my own daughter, you're the same age and gender. I also love Iva May." Her voice trailed off, and Bill figured she probably was thinking about Iva May's cancer and impending death. And how Kim would be without parents.

Maybe Bev was thinking to offer to be the mom since Iva May would be gone, but she didn't say.

"Well, I wasn't expecting to announce this to three people, but since you two might possibly be my parents..." Kim paused, looking at Bev, and then Bill, then back to Iva May. "I have some news of my own."

"You have cancer," Iva May said, the words seeming to slip out without her meaning them too.

Kim's eyes widened, and Bill feared the worst, before they narrowed and her brows crinkled. "No. What made you think that?"

"You've just been to the doctor's a good bit, and I know that to be tested and diagnosed and to choose a treatment plan takes a lot of appointments, and I figured it was cancer, since that ran in my family. Although...you might not be part of my family."

They were all quiet for just a moment thinking about the implications of that statement.

"It might be a good idea to take a DNA test, just for the health benefits. Not necessarily to determine parentage." Bev broke the silence that had descended.

Kim nodded, chewing on her lip.

"I know you said you needed time to process, but I just want you to know I'm not expecting you to call me dad or anything, but I'll do what I've always done and more if you want." Whatever it was that she needed to tell them, he wanted her to know he was in her corner.

They had spent a lot of holidays and birthdays together, so this wasn't too unusual, and Kim nodded thoughtfully.

"Maybe that DNA test would be a good idea. Because my news is I'm pregnant."

Chapter 9

B ev couldn't help herself. She gasped.

Kim had just gone through a divorce. It was final this past summer. Her daughter was out of high school. She'd been struggling, because the job that she had had been in her husband's company, and when he divorced her, he fired her and replaced her with the woman that he cheated on her with.

It had been nasty and terrible and all the awful things that anyone never wanted to have happen to them.

Iva May had cried multiple times over the pain her daughter had been going through. But there hadn't been anything that anyone could do. There usually wasn't in those kinds of situations, other than to sit and hold her hand, and just be there. And not be one of the people who abandoned her when she needed them most.

Bev had made sure that Iva May had been given money to give to Kim, and knowing what she knew about Bill, she guessed he'd done the same.

"So you made up with your husband?" Iva May asked slowly.

Kim looked at the floor, her head shaking slowly. She might be forty, but she was the same as people the world over, not wanting to disappoint her parent.

Bev held her breath.

"It was a one-night stand with a man I didn't know very well. I've not seen him since." She paused. "I'm three months along."

Bev managed to keep her face from showing her surprise, but the words were shocking. Kim wasn't the kind of woman to have a one-night stand. Iva May certainly hadn't raised her that way, and Kim had stayed with her husband, even though he was verbally abusive, self-centered, impossible to please, never grateful for anything, and only concerned about himself. He'd never been considerate or kind or even loving. Once he'd gotten Kim to marry him, he'd expected her to practically be a servant in their own home.

Kim hadn't wanted to be a statistic for their daughter and had insisted on looking on the bright side. She'd done her best to keep her vows, loving her husband, through more bad times than good. And raising her daughter to be considerate and kind, as much as she could.

"Then maybe the DNA test would be a good idea for the little one as well."

Kim nodded, a little bit of relief on her face at Bill's words. Maybe she'd been worried that they were going to reject her or lecture her. Bill's calm acceptance and unemotional reaction, looking immediately to what needed to be done and what was practical, rather than berating her, had given her peace.

Bev nodded and tried to imitate his unconcern. But she wanted to know why? And how? And who? And what in the world was Kim thinking?

"I was hoping I could move back home, Mom. I... I raised my daughter in Chicago, and I regret it. Blueberry Beach is the perfect town to raise a child. And you are the perfect example. I want her to know you."

Kim didn't need to say, "unlike my other daughter," who barely got to see her grandmother. Of course, this time around, Kim didn't have a husband who wouldn't let her go home to see her mother.

"I want you to come home." Iva May's words came out easily. But then her face froze, her eyes widened, and she sucked in a breath.

Bev moved to put a hand around her back. It was obvious that Iva May had completely forgotten about her own, terminal, cancer diagnosis.

"Actually, Kim, I have some...more...news of my own."

"What's that, Mom?" Kim said easily, although the curious look on her face morphed into concern as she saw Bev with her arm around Iva May and Bill moving to her other side.

"It's bad. What could it be? Wait. You thought I had cancer...because you do!" Kim cried out.

"It's terminal. They gave me six months to live. I'm meeting with hospice tomorrow."

"You need a second opinion. We need to fight this. We'll go to the new Blueberry Beach Hospital. They have all the latest technology. We're not going to let the cancer win." Kim's eyes moved from Bill to Bev and back again, pleading with them wordlessly to help her.

Iva May put her hand up. "I can get a second opinion, and in fact, I have been scheduled for that the same day as the hospice consultation. But," she continued, although Kim had opened her mouth to say something, "I saw the scans. There's so much cancer all through my body, everywhere. I don't want to do the kind of treatment that it would take in order to try to eliminate that, even if it could. The doctor said even if I did both chemo and radiation, it probably would only extend my life a little, and my quality of life would be terrible. That stuff makes you sick, and... I'm at peace."

"I'm not!" Kim exclaimed. "I want my daughter to know her grandmother."

"Maybe she will," Iva May said, sounding wise, as she looked pointedly from Kim to Bev. Her face melted into a smile, one of peace and of total contentment. "I'm not looking forward to dying, but I have always tried to keep my focus on heavenly things and remember that this world is not my final destination. That's where my treasure is. Everything I've been building, everything I've been doing has been with an eye toward what I have in heaven. And I'm kind of eager to go. Not that I want to die necessarily, but I'll see my mom. I miss her. I'll see aunts and uncles and grandparents."

Bev's throat tightened. Iva May looked so eager, and she truly did look like she was at peace. And who wouldn't want to go to see friends and loved ones?

"I want to see Jesus. I've spent almost every day of my life developing a friendship with him. I want to see him." She emphasized that last sentence. And there was no doubt she was sincere. "I'll see people I haven't seen in decades. People I've never met but only heard about. Don't be sad," she said, her hand coming out, reaching for Kim's, clasping it, and covering it with her other one. "Throw a party for me. This isn't the end. It's the beginning!"

"But I need you now. I don't know how to be a mother in my forties! I wasn't planning on bringing a child into the world, and especially without a dad. I'm scared."

Bev wanted to move forward, put her arms around Kim, and comfort her as a mother would. But she didn't move. This was Iva May's time with Kim. Maybe Bill and she shouldn't even be in the room. Although, maybe this was Iva May's way of easing the transition.

Her eyes, feeling heavy and sad, shifted to the man sitting across from her. His gaze was on her. Their eyes met.

He seemed just as sad, just as desperate to help, but he too seemed to realize that it wasn't his place. Not now.

Whatever happened with Iva May and whatever happened with the DNA test, Bill and she would be irrevocably connected through Kim and now Kim's baby. Because there was no way either one of them could abandon her now.

Lord? Did You do this for a specific reason? For me? For Bill? For the two of us to be together?

She hadn't wanted to go there. Hadn't wanted to do the whole relationship thing again.

But Bill is different. Different than any other man.

Even though he looked just like a normal man, with his balding head, his kind blue eyes, and the slightly paunchy stomach that many middle-aged men had.

He could be a million other men, except he had the character of one in a million.

Kim and Iva May had embraced and were holding each other while Kim cried quietly, and Iva May patted her back, looking sad but also totally peaceful.

"Let's give them some privacy," Bill said softly. He met Bev's eyes, and she nodded, then they both looked at Iva May who gave an almost imperceptible nod of her head.

Bev followed Bill out to the kitchen.

"Iva May did that on purpose, didn't she?" Bev said, needing his confirmation, although she was almost certain she was right.

"I'm pretty sure. That's the feeling I had, anyway."

"She didn't seem upset about Kim and the baby."

Bill shook his head. "I saw her eyes when Kim made that announcement. There was sadness there. I think mostly because she's going to miss out, never meeting her grandchild. But I think the same peace that she has with the cancer is helping her through this, too. I do think she knew exactly what she was doing." Bill paused, meeting her eyes, making sure she understood what he was talking about.

She did. Iva May finally told her secret, because she knew she wasn't going to be around for much longer, and she wanted Bill and Bev to be parents to Kim and her granddaughter and now this new baby, too.

"It's kind of funny the way the Lord works things out. Iva May hadn't even known about the baby, but it didn't matter. She felt the same way about that that she did about Kim and her other granddaughter."

"I was just sitting in there thinking the same thing. How God worked everything out so beautifully. With Iva May already planning to have Kim taken care of, learning about the baby didn't really upset her."

"No," Bev said thoughtfully. "There is also this...almost supernatural peace that seems to emanate off of her. I've heard of the Peace that Passes Understanding, but I think I saw it for the first time this morning in Iva May."

"I think you're right. I didn't consider that. She was calm, and I figured it was Jesus. He gives us peace when we need it. And seems like the end of our lives is definitely a time when we need it."

"So you really think there's no point in a second opinion?"

"I know God can do a miracle. But... Will He? Your guess is as good as mine."

Bill didn't sound like he thought for one second that God was going to extend Iva May's life. And that lack of confidence almost made Bev mad. Until she realized that probably the reason he didn't think God was going to was because He had given Iva May such peace about her passing. That He'd work things out and that Kim would be taken care of. And her baby. He didn't need to work a miracle, because He'd already brought things together so perfectly.

"Bev?"

She shook her head, having been lost in thought, and looked at Bill. "Yeah?"

"I... I know you're not interested..."

"We're going to be spending a lot of time together. At least, if Kim allows us to be her family, we could be together a good bit. Especially with this baby and Kim and me moving back to Blueberry Beach."

"Yeah. I..." He seemed to want to say something. It was unlike Bill to ever be unsure about anything. He always was wise and confident and quiet, but not doubtful or insecure. "You are the most amazing woman I've ever met. I loved you when you were a teenager, and I never stopped. I shouldn't have married my first wife, because it was apparent to her. Because I never stopped loving you. And I guess if you're going to be here permanently in Blueberry Beach, I just figured I'd like you to know that."

Bev's mouth opened. Bill was quiet, and normally he didn't go around talking about his feelings. It was extremely unusual for him to let them out like that.

She didn't know what to say.

Before she could get her mouth to form many words, Kim came out to the kitchen.

"Mom's feeling tired, so I helped her lie down on the couch where she could see the Christmas tree. The lights make her smile."

"They always have," Bev said faintly, remembering Iva May's almost childlike delight at Christmas decorations of any sort.

Kim nodded, her eyes red and filling again. She walked across the kitchen and pulled a tissue from the box on the counter. "How long have you guys known?"

"Your mom just told us yesterday," Bill said, and Bev figured he had chosen the words "your mom" deliberately. Letting Kim know that no one was trying to step in and take anything away from her.

"It's going to take me a little while to get used to this."

"We had all night and this morning. Take your time," Bill said.

"I've still not quite processed everything. It was definitely a shock to both of us as well," Bev added.

Kim blew her nose, then brushed her tears with the back of her hand. "Are you two together? I always thought you were perfect for each other. Mom said you used to be together. And I guess you were if you had me. Wouldn't that be funny? You two being my parents and having gotten together just at the time I need you." Kim laughed through her tears, then walked back over to the tissue box, grabbing another tissue and just standing beside the garbage can blowing her nose.

Bev's mouth hung open, and she couldn't stop her eyes as they followed Kim to the garbage can, then came back and landed on Bill who was looking at her. Quiet. Thoughtful. Not a hint of what he was thinking showing on his face.

But he didn't really need it to, because he had just told her he had loved her all his life.

"This doesn't really feel like Christmas," she whispered, more because she couldn't get any more force behind her words than because she wanted to keep anyone from hearing them. She had a hand at her throat, which didn't seem to want to work at all she realized as she tried to swallow.

"Definitely the weirdest Christmas I've ever had." Bill's gaze slanted toward the table. "At least the food should be good."

"I don't have any appetite."

"I'm not dead, so I have an appetite," Bill said, and there was a glint of humor in his eyes.

Her own widened. How could he be joking at a time like this?

"Iva May is at peace. She's not upset in the slightest. I think it's silly for us to be. After all, we love her. She knows we don't want her to go. But it's similar to your adult child moving out of your house. You don't want to see them go, but you don't want to hold them back from living the life that God has for them."

"But she's not living, she's dying," Bev said, realizing that Kim had turned around and was listening, but unable to pull her eyes from Bill long enough to look at Kim to see how she was taking this.

"She's not living on earth," Bill said. "But heaven is just beginning. She's looking forward to it. Who are we to hold her back? And who are we to be sad about it, if she's not?"

"You're right," Kim said, wonder in her voice like she'd never considered anything like that before. And she probably hadn't. Bev certainly hadn't.

"So yeah, it's not what I want, but a lot of my life hasn't been what I wanted, it's been what God thought was best for me. I'm not going to take this and complain about it. I'm going to make sure that when

I'm around Iva May, I'm making her last days everything that she wants them to be. That I'm not dragging her down, making her feel bad or guilty for leaving me behind, because that's what she's doing. We're staying, and she's graduating on to something new and better."

"And she deserves it. Because of the life she's led, because of the person she is. She deserves every good thing."

Bev nodded as Kim spoke.

"I guess that's the holiday we're celebrating? At least the beginning, because without Christ's birth, there couldn't have been death and atonement."

"Exactly. And we're witnessing it now. Iva May can look forward to where she's going, and we can look forward to joining her, because of the baby that was born today." Bill's words sparkled with confidence, even though they were soft. His eyes, no longer twinkling with humor, still had confidence and even happiness.

Bev figured it might be a little while before she was actually happy, but if the joy of the Lord was her strength, there should be joy somewhere, especially today, as they celebrated the birth of her Lord.

Kim walked across the kitchen, her hand on her stomach, and she stopped between Bill and Bev, looking at both of them. "I was a little standoffish when you spoke earlier about being a father, Bill. I... I'm sorry I wasn't more excited about it."

"Don't worry about it. You were shocked, as we were yesterday. I don't know how I would have reacted if you'd been here then. It took me some time to think about how I wanted to handle this news. Sometimes my first reaction isn't my best reaction."

"That's so true," Kim said, a bit of a smile on her face, like she'd definitely gone with her first reactions and wished she hadn't. "Regardless, whether we do the DNA testing or whether we don't, whatever you guys want to be in my life, I want you in it."

She turned to Bill. "Your wisdom, the way you see things, the way you're always around to help people, I want to be like that."

She looked at him for just a second before she turned to Bev. "Your self-control, your class, and your integrity are all things I look at and admire. I want to be like you two." She grunted a little. "At forty, you'd think I'd have more of all of those things, but—"

"You do. You have all of those things and more. Don't sell yourself short, just because you made a mistake. Just because life hasn't been what you wanted it to be for the last year. You've gone through a really hard time, and you handled it with class and with integrity."

"Not integrity. I had one night that had nothing to do with integrity and everything to do with stupidity."

"Don't talk like that," Bev said quickly. "Or at least, I guess we all make stupid mistakes, just admit it. Move on. Because God has a way of taking our stupid mistakes and turning them into really great lessons and even better blessings. As long as we admit that they were mistakes, repent, and turn to Him, He can make beauty out of ashes. That's almost His specialty."

Bev smiled, thinking about the baby in the manger, the stable, and the poverty that he had been born into, and how God had made something so beautiful and so precious out of what seemed like nothing.

And that's when she knew, truly knew, that everything was going to be okay, even though Iva May was going to be leaving them. With her dying breaths, she'd forged a family. And now Bev just needed to figure out a way to see if she and Bill might be able to pick up the pieces that they had and make something beautiful out of them, too.

Chapter 10

B ill walked slowly through the public parking lot at the end of Main Street on Blueberry Beach, heading toward the lake.

He wasn't going to walk on the beach. It was too cold for that. The frigid wind would drive him inside, but he needed some time to think. Needed to remember how small he was, especially compared to the vastness of God.

For a few moments today, it had actually felt like Christmas. He'd forgotten Iva May's cancer, although every time he looked at her, she looked more and more tired. Forgotten all the mystery surrounding Kim's baby and her unusual one-night stand.

Forgotten that he'd bared his heart to Bev, done what he needed to do, allowed his feelings to show, and she basically brushed them off.

It hurt. He wanted to leave, to go back to his shop, his lonely apartment where his feelings were protected, and no one pushed him to take chances, and no one rejected him.

Beyond Iva May's hospice appointment in the morning, which would be surreal at best, but he promised to be there, it was the idea that he'd tried with Bev, she hadn't been interested, and now he needed to just accept that.

Stopping at the edge of the pier, he looked over the beach and out into the vast black water, listening to the waves crash against the shore. There was a stiff breeze - there almost always was - but the lake was relatively calm, and the waves sounded soothing, not angry. Befitting the spirit of Christmas.

He supposed there were people who couldn't imagine the beach at Christmas and who couldn't imagine he'd made a habit over the years of always standing along the edge, if not walking along the shore, just thinking about the goodness of God, and the baby in the manger, and the privilege that he had of living in one of the most beautiful places on earth.

Even if it was a little cold.

He laughed to himself as he shoved his hands deeper into his pockets and lifted his shoulders so his coat covered his neck.

The older he got, the more susceptible he was to the cold.

And that was another thing that Iva May's appointment in the morning reminded him. He wasn't getting younger. He turned sixty this past year. His fellow shop members had made a big celebration, and he'd gone along with it, but inside, he wondered what the point was.

He didn't have a wife, didn't have children, and felt like it was too late in any event now. What woman would want an old man like him anyway?

Plus, he'd already married one woman hoping to forget Bev, and that had been a disaster. He thought he'd been devoted to his wife, had treated her the best way he knew how, had never mentioned Bev's name or allowed himself to think about her while he was married, and it hadn't been enough.

Maybe he was just destined to be single and lonely for whatever years he had left.

Normally he didn't allow himself such morose thoughts. Normally he tried to look on the bright side of everything, look at things the way God did, to see his life in light of eternity. Having a wife, having a family wasn't the end goal of his life. It was to praise and glorify God. If God thought he could do that better with a wife, God would give him one.

And if God thought he could do it better without, then that's what he needed to do. Most of the time, he could remind himself to keep his eyes on Jesus, remember the things that were important—doing God's will, bringing glory to God—and he didn't think too much about his lonely life and his longing to have someone to share it with.

Lord? Haven't I done everything You've asked? Didn't You make me to desire a wife? To need one? Have I missed her somehow?

Silence except for the crashing of the waves down at the beach. Then the stiff breeze swishing by his ears.

Pulling a hand out of his pocket, he moved his beanie further down on his head, covering his ears entirely, then shoving his hand back into his coat.

He couldn't help thinking about how nice it would be to have a woman standing beside him, standing close, sharing heat, looking forward to going back to his apartment and sitting under the twinkling Christmas lights, drinking hot chocolate and eating candy and nuts, and talking about the Christmases that they'd shared together.

"It's pretty cold out to be standing here," a voice interrupted his thoughts, and he turned more quickly than he meant to.

"Pastor Kane. I could say the same thing to you."

Pastor Kane was dressed very similarly to him, with a beanie cap on his head and heavy winter jacket with his hands shoved deep in the pockets.

"Where's your wife?" Bill asked, not just because he'd been thinking about his longing for a wife, but because it was Christmas and if there was ever a day to spend with your wife, this was it.

"We have some kids from the children's center at home, and she's watching them. She promised them a movie before they went to bed, so I didn't leave her with any extra work." Pastor Kane's lips curved up under his two-day stubble. Like somehow Bill might judge him for leaving his wife with the kids while he went to take a walk.

"That seems like a nice family thing to do on a Christmas evening. Watch a movie," Bill murmured.

"I thought so too, but I looked out the window and saw you walking down the street, and thought I'd come out and see if you had somewhere to go. You're welcome to join us if you'd like?" Pastor Kane's offer was a question, but Bill was shaking his head before he got it completely out.

"No. I've been at Iva May's all day with Bev and Kim. I've had plenty of company." His longing for a wife wasn't a longing for social interaction. It was a longing for someone who understood him at the soul level. He wasn't lonely for people, he was lonely for a person. Just one. Unless they had children. Which, he'd already established the fact that he was sixty years old and wouldn't be having more children.

"Christmas is a hard day to spend alone," Pastor Kane said, almost as though Bill had not just said that he hadn't spent it alone.

But then he realized that maybe Pastor Kane knew exactly what he was talking about, since he had just recently gotten married and knew what it was like to spend Christmas by himself. With people, but not with his soul mate.

"It definitely gives you a longing for a wife. Kids." Normally Bill wouldn't have said anything like that, but he was so discouraged at opening himself up for Bev and having it amount to nothing that maybe he was looking for someone to actually care.

"You have someone in mind?" Pastor Kane said casually, facing the water, not looking at Bill.

Iva May hadn't said they couldn't tell anyone, and he and Bev hadn't talked about it, but Pastor Kane was used to people's confidences, and so Bill said, "I don't know if Iva May and Bev are going to want this to get out, but Iva May told us yesterday that Kim might be our child."

"You and Bev?" Pastor Kane said, as though he couldn't believe it, had never thought of them together.

Bill shoved his hands even deeper in his pockets, tense. Was it so unbelievable that an old man like him could catch the eye of someone as beautiful and accomplished as Bev? Of course, back when she was a teenager, she wasn't accomplished, although she was still beautiful.

"Yeah. For a little while, we saw each other, but she never wanted to tell anyone, so we kept our relationship hidden, and most people don't know."

"I vaguely remember someone saying something about Bev being pregnant when she was a teen. She lost the baby, if I recall the story correctly. Was that yours?" Pastor Kane was way too astute, and Bill shifted.

"Yes."

"That's funny. I've never heard you mentioned in connection with that story. At all."

Bill breathed out, pushing against the wind, feeling the cold cut into his face, somehow sharpening his thoughts. "She was fifteen. I was twenty. If she had told people who the father was, I could have gone to jail."

There were several beats of silence before Pastor Kane said, "That's why you two kept your relationship quiet?"

"That's why she wanted to. She told me she was eighteen, and I hadn't seen the need to keep things quiet. I just went along with it because she wanted to. She didn't admit her real age until she was pregnant and I wanted to get married."

"I see. You resented being lied to?"

"No! She did it to protect me. I've never seen her utter another lie. I suppose, in my youthful stupidity, I admired her for wanting to protect me."

"But your relationship just couldn't last through the loss of the baby?"

"I guess." He wasn't sure whether to go into the whole thing with Darla. "She believed some rumors about me, and she broke it off. She said she didn't want me, and that was it."

"You didn't fight for her?"

"I couldn't."

"Why not?" Pastor Kane acted like Bill was the one in the wrong. But he'd only done what she asked; he hadn't been able to do more.

"Because she was fifteen. If I'd been around her, people might have suspected that her baby was mine. She told me she didn't love me anyway. That she had bigger plans than just being barefoot and pregnant for the rest of her life." Bill grunted. "Then with Darla claiming that she and I were together, I think that just gave Bev a reason to ditch me."

"You still love her."

"Yeah. Never stopped."

"Isn't that funny? Sometimes we fall in love one time, and that's it. There's just never anyone else."

"I tried. Tried with Mardi. I didn't allow myself to think about Bev, I never tried to find anything out about Bev or talk about her. I was as devoted as I could be to my wife. But it wasn't enough."

Funny that once a man started baring his soul, he seemed to want to do it to anyone who would listen.

"From what I heard, you were a great provider but maybe a little closed off emotionally."

Closed off emotionally? What? Was he supposed to be a touchy-feely, Cupid-type person?

It was one thing for him to think it about himself but a completely different story for people to say it about him.

He tried not to take offense and keep his voice level when he said, "What do you mean, closed off emotionally?"

"I don't know. Just the way a lot of men are. Like, I told you I loved you once, if anything changes, I'll let you know, kind of thing."

Bill bit his tongue. He wanted to deny it immediately. Because he had told Mardi that he loved her. On their anniversary. On Valentine's Day. Probably on Christmas, although he couldn't remember.

"Mardi knew I loved her."

"Did she?"

"I know she did. I didn't just tell her once on her wedding day and then never again."

"Did you tell her every day?"

"If I tell her every day, it would get old. It would just seem like something you say but don't really mean. There wouldn't be any meaning behind it."

"Maybe that's the way you feel, but maybe she needed to hear it every day."

Bill turned his head toward Kane, who still was looking at him. "Are you serious?"

Chapter 11

Kane slowly nodded his head. "I am. Some women need to hear that. Often. More than once a day. She might need to know that you think she's beautiful. And you can't just tell her that once either. And you have to think she's beautiful when she wakes up in the morning, when she thinks she's ugly, and when she sees her flaws and imperfections, you let her know that none of that stuff matters to you."

"But I never complained about anything. I don't even remember if she had any flaws. I always let my actions speak louder than my words."

Pastor Kane chuckled just a little, then shook his head, turning back out toward the lake. "Sometimes people don't read into your actions what you think they do. Sometimes, you're better off saying, 'I grabbed groceries for you, because I love you and I wanted to make your life easier. I expanded the store, because I love you and I was hoping to make a little more money for us.' Or 'I brought you a candy bar because I love you, and I know you love them.' Or 'I think you're beautiful,' and when she starts pointing out all her flaws, you say, 'you might see them as imperfections, but I see them as part of the woman I love, and that makes them beautiful to me.'"

Bill had stopped pretending to stare out at the water and faced Pastor Kane as he spoke. He'd never said anything like any of that to Mardi. Or to Bev, not that he and Bev had spent much time together. But it hadn't even occurred to him that he might need to repeat himself over and over again. To say why he brought home the groceries, or why he worked late at the store, or why he drove them to town when he'd rather stay home. It was because he loved them.

"Are you serious? Daily?"

Pastor Kane didn't look at him but just nodded at the lake. "Yeah. I don't know what it is about women. They're more in their heads than we are, I guess. Or maybe they just need to be reassured. They don't look at us and say, 'he's still here, he must still love me.' They look at us and think, 'he's still here, but does he wish he was somewhere else? He's still here, but is he thinking about leaving? He's still here, but maybe he's here out of duty and not because he loves me.' You know, all of those things."

"No. I didn't know. Women think like that?"

"All the time."

"All women?"

"It's really hard to put a blanket statement over everything, but in a general sense, yeah. They want to hear you love them. They want to know—hear and see—that they're still the most important one to you. And just so you don't get the mistaken idea that I'm telling you that you just need to tell them, and that's good enough, your actions have to back it up. If you say, 'you are the most important one,' and then you deliver groceries to the neighbor lady and forget about the list your wife handed you, or if you tell her that you love her, and that she's important to you, the most important one, but then you don't change the oil in your wife's car until the neighbor lady asks you to change the oil in hers, or you take their advice and ignore what your wife says, or..." Pastor Kane's voice trailed off like he was having trouble coming up with examples.

But Bill's mind was working on it. Trying to remember if that was how he treated Mardi. Had his actions shown that she was the most important thing to him? Or had he put his business—or even Iva May or someone else—first?

"Basically, if I tell her that she's the most important thing, she's going to be looking for my actions to back that up."

"Absolutely. You can say it, but if you don't act it, then it means nothing. Some women don't even need to hear you say it, they just need to see the actions. They're going to understand that when the neighbor asks you to go to a concert with them and offers you a free ticket, and you decline, because you know it's something your wife wants to do, so you purchase two tickets instead of going for free with your neighbor, just so your wife can go, not spending more time golfing with your buddies than you spend with your wife... Actually, that shouldn't be equal. You should spend far, far more of your free time with your wife than you do with your buddies or anyone else... Stuff like that."

He appreciated Pastor Kane knowing he needed concrete examples. But something Pastor Kane had said had triggered the idea that...he had money, his inheritance, and he had never used it on himself or his family.

Of course, before they got married, Mardi had known all about it. It's not like he hid it. But he'd also told her the money had been earmarked by him, not stipulations of his inheritance, to be used to benefit others.

And had she felt like he wasn't making her important when he didn't spend that money on her?

It was a question he'd probably never get an answer to. Mardi was married to someone else, and they didn't exactly talk.

Maybe she resented the fact that they lived on a small shop owner's salary when he had millions of dollars in his bank account.

That was water under the bridge, but if he could see what he had done wrong, instead of thinking that everything was Mardi's fault, maybe he would have more of a chance with Bev.

"Bev is going to need you to open up to her. I think especially since she's been in the business world and been double-crossed, even had someone marry her for her money. That's going to make it harder, and she's going to need to hear you and see your actions follow up what you say."

Bill hunched over even more, not necessarily because of the wind, but more because he wanted to draw into himself at the idea of having to expose himself even more than what he already had.

He appreciated Pastor Kane's insight, though. Insight Bill knew had been gained from counseling couples over the years.

"I might do all of that, and she might not take me anyway."

"That's true." Pastor Kane nodded his head, very matter-of-factly.

He didn't say anything else, just let that statement hang there, and seemed to be waiting on Bill to think it through.

Bill almost laughed. Pastor Kane might as well have asked, is she worth it?

Was Bev worth taking the risk? Did he want her bad enough to open himself up to the risk of rejection? A painful rejection if he pursued her as boldly as Pastor Kane seemed to suggest he should. Opening himself up, letting his emotions show, telling her how he felt, acting on those words.

All scary things, except for maybe the actions. He was an action kind of guy, not the kind of guy who got all touchy-feely with his emotions.

"You know, the people in this town have benefited greatly from your wisdom. You haven't held anything back, not in your knowledge and not in any way that you could help anyone. I think the town of Blueberry Beach appreciates that." Pastor Kane spoke carefully. "So you didn't really ask for any advice, but I thought I might give you some anyway."

"Please. I'd love any advice you have for me."

"I know you're sixty because I went to your birthday party this past year." There was humor in Pastor Kane's voice.

"Yeah, the whole town knows my age. I guess I don't care."

"And you've been doing the same thing for sixty years, more or less, and you know what your results are."

"True."

"You know what you want, or maybe I should say who you want, and you know what *hasn't* worked in the past."

He wanted Bev. He always had. Pastor Kane was right, he'd never fought for her, never pursued her, never chased after her and let her know exactly how much she meant to him and how much he wanted her. Not once.

And even with Mardi, he'd let her go. He hadn't fought to keep her. He hadn't even really fought to pursue her. She'd been the one to ask him out, and his proposal had kind of been the "hey, how about we get married" kind of thing and not a big deal that had told her how special she was to him.

"If you want new results, you have to do things a new way. You know the old saying where you can't keep doing the same old thing and expect new results?"

"I know."

"I'm not knocking consistency, because I think that's important. And going to work day in and day out, just doing what you're supposed to do, sticking with your job, being who you are. That's all important, and I'm not suggesting you change that. But if you want to be married, if you want the opportunity to have the girl you've always wanted, you have to go after that with both hands. You have to be willing to take risks. To let go of the sarcasm and be real. To show your emotions. Be willing to be rejected, and maybe multiple times."

Bill knew Bev was worth it. Truly, but the idea of getting out of his comfortable routine, especially since he'd already been rejected once. The idea of being rejected more, of letting her know he still wanted her, even when she didn't want him, of being kind and showing romantic gestures when she didn't return them, just felt scary.

"You don't want what you do to become harassment. There's a fine line there now, but women do appreciate being pursued. They appreciate knowing that they're worth your time and effort, they're worth the risk." Pastor Kane grunted. "That's where a lot of men go wrong after they get married. It's like they've already gotten her, they kind of put her on a shelf, put a checkmark by her name, accomplished that, and they go on to other things, and they forget, or maybe they don't know to begin with, that part of what she loved about you was the fact that you made her feel special and valuable and worth the time and effort it took to find her and keep her happy."

"Well, I suppose if I get married, I'll be back for some marriage counseling or advice on keeping a good relationship."

"You can come on back, but it's probably going to sound real simple, because it's basically, you have to put her first, before yourself, even, and *she needs to know it*. And you just have to be kind."

"That sounds simple."

"It is. Sometimes kindness is hard."

"I'm sorry you had to work on a holiday." Bill shifted, figuring he probably had enough stuff to think about, enough new things he needed to try to do. Enough changes to make in his life. Enough thoughts and ideas of how to win Bev.

"It's not really work. Plus, Christmas is kind of the reason I have a job."

"I feel like I should pay you," Bill said after he laughed.

"Nah." Pastor Kane pulled his hand out of his pocket and waved it dismissively. "The best payment would be to see you two together forever. I can't think of anything else more worthwhile."

"You and me both." Bill didn't mean to sound wishful, but he figured he probably did. It would pretty much be a dream come true, but sometimes a man had to get out of his comfort zone in order to take steps to make his dreams come true.

Maybe that's what he needed to do.

"On a completely different subject, mind if I ask a question?" Pastor Kane asked, a little hesitantly.

"No. Of course not. Go on." It must be something pretty heavy if Pastor Kane asked if he could ask a question. Bill felt a twist of nervousness roll in his stomach.

"I talked to Iva May. She actually called me last week, and I was praying for the outcome of her test."

"I'm glad she's talking to you about it."

"Me too. It's always helpful to know when any of my congregants need prayer." Pastor Kane took a breath. "I've handled a lot of people who've been given a terminal diagnosis, who are facing the possibility of death. But I've never had one so at peace with it like Iva May. I... I guess I'm betraying a bit of a confidence, or maybe asking you to, but I was wondering if she's really as secure as she seems?"

"She is. She's rock solid. She actually seems like she's taking her eyes off of earth and putting them on heaven and making her focus there. I think she's ready to go right now."

"I see. That's the impression I got as well, and I love it. What an example."

"It sure is."

"Well, thank you. I... I just didn't want to walk into her house, smiling and happy for her, if that wasn't truly the way she felt."

"It is, and it's been a blessing to Kim and to Bev, and I know it's been a blessing to me. It's changed our attitudes. It's hard to be sad when her whole desire is for us to be happy for her."

"Yeah, definitely the attitude of the person who is dying is a big determination on how people feel about it."

"She's always been submissive to God and willing to do whatever He wants. And in the way she's seeing it, this is just one more thing He wants from her, and she's going to do it to the best of her ability. I really admire that."

"I do too. I feel like she ought to be preaching sermons on Sunday."

They chuckled a little, and Bill appreciated Pastor Kane's humanness. That he didn't try to put on a show that he was holier than anyone else or more spiritual. But was honest about his shortcomings. And didn't try to hide the fact that he was flawed along with everyone else.

"I'll definitely not be afraid to smile."

"Don't. I think she appreciates it. Although she's tired, more tired than I've ever seen her, and it's almost shocking to see the change in her today versus even last week when I saw her."

"If she's ready to go, maybe it won't be long." Pastor Kane shifted, almost as though he were getting ready to walk away. Then he stopped. "I believe tomorrow is her meeting with hospice?"

"It is."

"Is anyone going to be there with her?"

"Kim. And she asked Bev and me to be there as well."

Bill didn't miss the grin on Pastor Kane's face when he mentioned that Bev and he were going to be together tomorrow. Pastor Kane didn't need to tell him that here was an opportunity for him to do something different, rather than the same things he'd always done.

Instead, Pastor Kane clasped him on the shoulder and said, "Thanks for chatting. Merry Christmas."

"Thanks for the wisdom. Merry Christmas to you, too."

Chapter 12

"All right, we'll watch for your emails with all the information and be expecting you to start sending someone in later this week," Kim said as she walked the hospice representative to the door.

Iva May, who hadn't gotten out of her chair since Bev had arrived, barely even acknowledged the woman was leaving.

Bev tried to shove down some of her panic and fear. Iva May had seemed tired yesterday, but Bev had chalked that up to the excitement of Christmas and having Kim come home.

But today, she not only seemed tired, she seemed a little confused. Or... Maybe not confused, just lethargic. Not herself.

Normally, she would never allow anyone to walk out of her house on their own. She would have been chatting with them as they left, asking about their family and their own health and all the things that Iva May talked to people about that helped her see where she could be the biggest blessing in their life.

Bev lifted her eyes and saw Bill staring at her.

There had been something different about him today, too.

It was obvious to her that he had come to terms, and had complete peace, with Iva May's condition. He hadn't seemed bothered by the questions the hospice representative had asked. Ones like, will you need a shower chair? How about a wheelchair? Do you have funeral plans in place? A living will?

He hadn't batted an eyelash when they'd said that their purpose was to have her die with dignity, at home, as she had expressed her desire to do, and that calling an ambulance could interfere with that because once she was in the hospital, and they started lifesaving measures, like IVs and respirators, it might be difficult to get her home again.

Bev had taken that to mean that when Iva May was dying, they shouldn't panic and call 911, because that's what she was supposed to be doing. Dying.

At that point, she'd had to get up and leave the room for a moment.

Not that it hadn't felt real yesterday, but it had felt more nebulous, further in the future, like they had time.

Today, Iva May's death was like a slap in the face. Right there. Something she couldn't miss. Something that hurt. Something that she wanted to do something about but couldn't.

"It's a matter of admitting that death is God's decision, not ours. And knowing that not only is she going to be happier where she's going, but she's going to be happier if she sees us happy and not grieving." Bill's eyes held concern as he tried to hold her gaze. She hadn't asked him to talk, hadn't asked a question at all, he'd just spoken.

Maybe on a good day, she might have wondered how he was able to read her mind so well, but today that thought didn't even occur to her. She just appreciated his solid, steady presence. Because she pretty much felt like she wanted to fall apart. Nothing in the business world had prepared her for this.

"I don't like to think about death at all," she said quietly, aware that Iva May sat in the chair just feet from them, even though her eyes were closed and she snored softly.

Kim seemed to be in deep conversation with the hospice nurse, since she could hear their voices drifting down the hall.

The Christmas lights twinkled, almost spitefully, or maybe mocking Bev, saying, *you're supposed to be happy*.

She wanted to rip them down. Wanted to take them outside and stomp on them, stomp on the idea that anybody, or anything, could be happy right now. Not when Iva May was leaving them forever.

"Something we all have to do." Bill's words were soft, gentle. Exactly the kind of tone Bev needed, as much as she didn't want to admit it.

"We might as well look at good examples and think about how we want to die."

"You can do that if you want to. I'm going to go kicking and screaming," she muttered.

She didn't expect Bill's snort of laughter. "That sounds like you."

She smiled too, but she wasn't sure it was a compliment. After all, they were supposed to meekly accept whatever God had ordained for their life. She'd never been very good at meekly accepting anything. In fact, meek wasn't necessarily a word that anyone would use to describe her personality.

Over the last decade, she'd realized that and had been working on it. But in her experience in the business world, meek people got run over. It was the people who went after what they wanted, who made sure to toot their own horns, who never tooted anyone else's horn louder than their own, and who put on a show for the right people, who got ahead.

As someone who was in charge of a huge corporation, she knew that. After all, those were people she noticed.

"What you said about submitting to God, it's something I've been working on," she finally admitted. Just because Bill felt safe.

"Bev? Bill?" Kim stuck her head in the room.

They both looked up, and Bev said, "Yes?"

"It looks like Mom is sleeping, and if you guys don't mind, I'm gonna take a walk."

"That's fine. We'll be here."

"I was thinking that maybe we could hash out a bit of a schedule so she's not ever alone? Maybe we can do that when you get back?" Bill said, and Bev wanted to smack her head. She should have been the one to think about that. She should have been instigating it, too. After all, she was the go-getter in the group.

She hadn't even thought of it. Hadn't even considered they couldn't all just sit here and watch Iva May die hour upon hour, day upon day, week upon week...however long it took. They had lives to live, houses that needed to be taken care of. And she had to do a few things with her business.

Although those things seemed very unimportant right now.

Kim ducked back out, and Bill moved in his chair, just a little, but enough that his body was in a position where he could reach across the little table and put his hand over top of Bev's. His touch was warm and comforting, and she was tempted to turn her hand over and thread their fingers together.

Somehow, when she was around Bill, the idea of depending on him scared her. Depending on people had never been something that had worked out for her.

She almost pulled her hand away but couldn't. It felt too good.

"You've grown. A lot since we were younger, obviously, but especially in the last five or ten years. I've noticed a difference every time you've been in town."

"That's funny since I've made a point to avoid you when I was in town."

"I wondered if that's why I had to go out of my way in order to see you." Bill didn't seem angry; in fact, his lips held a little bit of a smile.

"You're not offended that I avoided you?"

"Maybe a little hurt," Bill said, slowly, like those weren't words he would normally say, and Bev had to agree. No one liked to admit that they were hurt. It was showing weakness. "But I also get it. I wasn't the person that you wanted to be face-to-face with all the time."

"No. Is it wrong for me to want my past to stay in my past?"

"I guess not. Some might say that's a smart idea, unless revisiting your past has the potential to make your future better. Then it might be a good idea."

He seemed to have a message in those words, beyond the surface, and she narrowed her eyes at him.

"You're saying a friendship with you would make me better?"

"A friendship. A romance. Possibly marriage, but I don't want to scare you."

She opened her mouth to say that marriage was scary, and he couldn't utter that word without striking fear in her heart, but it wouldn't have been entirely true. Marriage in general scared her, yes. Because it was an irrevocable covenant. One she'd been in, one she hadn't enjoyed, one she was glad to be free from.

But she'd made an irrevocable contract with a man who had no character.

Making such a covenant with a man like Bill...yeah. That could improve her future.

So she kept her mouth shut.

Bill squeezed her hand, just a gentle tightening of his fingers, and she lifted her eyes to his, realizing that maybe it would be rude of her to not say anything, since maybe she should, wanted, to respond to the olive branch he'd offered.

"Friendship. I'd welcome that. I really would."

"Then it's done."

Maybe it was that simple for him. She believed it probably was. He'd be loyal to her to his dying day from this point on, she had no doubt. No matter what she did or what she said.

For her, it was slightly more complicated. She didn't want to give her loyalty that easily and that quickly. Even though it was Bill, and she knew he wouldn't abuse it.

Too many other people already had.

"Friends?" she said, lifting her lips a little. Fighting through the reluctance. After all, she just admitted to herself that Bill wouldn't abuse her loyalty. Just because other people had was no reason to punish him.

"And working toward more," he said, that same grin lifting his lips and giving her stomach something that felt like butterflies but couldn't possibly be. She'd been fifteen the last time a man's smile gave her butterflies, and look how that had turned out for her.

"Do you think Kim is ours?" she asked, and if he didn't understand where her change of subject came from, he didn't let on.

"I can see your eyes in her. In fact, I was looking at her picture..." He nodded his head at the wall, where a grouping of pictures hung above the couch. In Bev's grief and shock, she hadn't even remembered them, hadn't thought to look at them. "And maybe my memory is faulty, but Kim's teenage picture looks exactly like you, just with a different hairstyle."

Standing slowly, she walked over to the pictures, skipping through the baby pictures and landing on one that was almost certainly a high school graduation picture.

There was no doubt as to the resemblance.

"You're right. I have one that looks very similar to this. I think we're even in the same position."

"It's that little grin. Confident and serious but at the same time, there is just a hint of flirting. You always got me with that grin."

Bev turned, not meaning to grin that grin he had just described, but she knew what was on her lips anyway. "Is that so?"

He smiled, a self-effacing smile that told her that he hadn't been joking. "That's the grin. It's the one that could get me to do whatever you wanted me to."

She shook her head, laughing a little, turning back to the pictures, but she thought he was probably right. He had never told her no. Not for long.

Somehow, he managed to make her forget about everything, her fear, even her panic and hopelessness. He filled her chest with warmth and made her heart lighter with just a few comments, compliments.

She wasn't a teenager, and Bill certainly wasn't a young man anymore, but he kind of made her forget that too.

Plus, as much as she liked the young man Bill, she appreciated this older, more mature, wiser, and...more emotional Bill.

Staring at the picture, it took a few minutes for her mind to come back to what she'd gone over for to begin with. Her daughter hadn't died. She'd just been switched.

"Kim is ours," she said, turning back and facing Bill square on.

He nodded. He'd come to that realization himself, from the lack of surprise or astonishment on his face.

"I'm not sure she completely believes that yet," he added.

"She may never believe it," Bev murmured.

Bill nodded. "I can't blame her. Iva May is an amazing woman. And now that she's leaving us, if it were me, I might feel a little bit like I'm betraying my mother to even think that I have other parents. You know?"

Bev nodded. She hadn't thought of that, but she could see it. After all, Iva May was the one who had made all the sacrifices in raising Kim. And Kim knew exactly what those sacrifices were, since she'd raised a daughter as well.

"But this new baby... Whether she admits that we're her parents or not, I feel like she needs us."

"Me too. I mean, starting over is hard enough on your own, at forty. But starting over pregnant, while recovering from such a huge wound from her husband, feels impossible to me, and it didn't even happen to me."

Bev's heart hurt; it would hurt even if she hadn't believed that Kim was her daughter, but the jumble of emotions from finding out she had a daughter and knowing how badly her daughter had been hurt, and how much she needed her, just made everything feel so big and sticky and crunchy in her chest.

"I really want to grab ahold of someone. I felt like that even before I knew Kim was ours. It makes me so angry to think that her husband thinks it's okay to treat someone like that, to treat my daughter like that." Bill's voice held suppressed anger, although he hadn't moved from his seat, and he still looked relaxed.

She'd always admired his self-control. She supposed that with self-control came a lack of feeling. And maybe that was why he hadn't fought her when she believed the rumors about him cheating and broke up with him.

"There's nothing we can do about that. At least not on a personal level. I've actually already started a few things on a business level, but it will take a while to see the effects."

"Nothing illegal."

She pursed her lips, holding her smile in. "Nothing illegal. I'm shocked you'd even suggest such a thing."

And there she was, smiling again, because of Bill.

"This morning, on my way here, I felt like this was going to be one of the hardest days of my life. And I was looking at weeks if not months of more difficulties. You...helped me. Made me smile. Lightened my heart and took my thoughts in a new direction. I appreciate it."

Bill tilted his head, his shoulders tensing just a little but his words easy. "That's what friends are for."

"You two should be more than friends." Iva May's raspy voice came from her chair.

Bev's eyes shifted. Iva May's eyes weren't open, but there was no doubt she had spoken.

"Trying to talk her into it, Miss Iva May. Give me some time."

"I don't have much time."

Bill's shoulders shrugged as he stood, moving over to her chair and kneeling down beside it, holding her hand. "I don't want to rush. She needs to choose me because she wants me, not because she feels pressure."

Iva May's eyes cracked, and they landed on Bill. "Why do you always have to be so smart?"

Bev walked over, kneeling down on the other side of Iva May's chair. "Are you hungry? Can I get you something to eat or drink?"

Iva May's brows furrowed, almost as though the question was a hard one, and she had to think about it.

"I guess I could take some yogurt. Maybe a little apple juice if we have it."

"We have the yogurt," Bill said. "And I can go to the store and get apple juice. Is there anything else?"

Bev loved the tenderness in his voice, the care and concern, the way he wasn't afraid to kneel and take Iva May's hand, to help with whatever she needed.

Iva May shook her head, almost as though she were too tired to say anything more.

"Do you mind if we arrange the furniture a little bit?" Bill asked her gently when she didn't say anything else.

"Do what you need to," Iva May said slowly but without hesitation, giving Bev the idea that she truly didn't care what they did.

"I just want to make things a little easier so we can sit beside you without kneeling on the floor. So we have a table right here we can keep the things that we need for you and keep anything that you might want close by."

"It's fine. The only thing I want close by are my people. You do what's easiest for you after that."

Those words made Bev's throat tighten. It was so much like Iva May to be more concerned about the people around her than anything that might make her comfortable or happy. In fact, *things* really didn't make Iva May happy. It was always people. Or maybe just a radiance that shone from her inside.

"How about you move one of those chairs over here, and I'll move the card table over beside it. When I get back from the store, we can rearrange things so that they are a little bit handier and so that she can have two people sitting beside her and still have the card table nearby."

"That sounds good. It might make sense to move the couch and put her chair in its place, at least until they get the hospital bed here."

"They said it would be delivered tomorrow, but I'm guessing she'll have a lot of visitors, and it would be nice if they were able to be close enough to hold her hand. I'm sure she would appreciate it."

"Where should we put the hospital bed?" Bev asked, still feeling like everything was a little surreal that she was even talking about this kind of stuff.

"I think we should put it right in the middle of the floor. That way we can have chairs on either side, the table maybe even behind the head of the bed—there's enough room—and everything we need right where we need it. It's silly to make things harder on ourselves to try to make it look good, but maybe that's my male brain speaking."

"It would be different if this were going to be the new way we decorate her living room, but it's not." Bev took a breath. "I agree with you. Let's make it so it's easy on the people who are caring for her and the people who want to visit and make it easy for Iva May to have what she needs."

She couldn't believe how well she was handling this. But it almost certainly had to do with Iva May's attitude and Bill's quiet strength. Funny, how the people around a person affected that person. And she realized anew how important friends were. And how susceptible she'd been to the way her business associates had acted. Although she'd never done anything illegal or immoral, she'd allowed their attitudes of wanting to get ahead and wanting to put their best foot forward to affect her and make her be concerned about how she looked and the bottom line, sometimes over the people around her and what God might want for her.

Knowing they were all here working to help each other made it easier to do what she needed to.

Chapter 13

"What are you doing?" Bev stopped short as she walked into Iva May's kitchen where Bill stood with a tool belt around his waist, the kitchen devoid of tables and chairs and with what seemed like hundreds of sparkly stars hanging from the ceiling.

Bill straightened, eyeing her uncertainly, like he wasn't sure what her reaction was going to be. "Kim and I talked to Iva May last night after you left; she was up until after midnight."

It was no wonder, since she had slept most of the day after the visit with the doctor for the second opinion. He had said the same thing as the first doctor. Only, after having examined Iva May and seen her physical decline, he said six months was probably an optimistic estimate.

"They're delivering the bed today, and Iva May said she'd love to be in the kitchen because of the brightness and being able to look outside the big windows and the sliding glass door over here." Bill nodded toward the door that opened up on her side porch. Bev had eaten there many times during the summers, enjoying the lake breeze and the beautiful Michigan summer sky. It was a happy place. No wonder Iva May wanted to be able to look out on it.

There were lots of memories attached to it, too.

"So you remodeled her kitchen?" she said, still not entirely on board with what they were doing.

"I just removed the chairs and the table and put up the stars that Kim had brought for her. Iva May has always loved to lie down in her yard and look at the stars."

"I think she'd want us to put her hospital bed outside if it were summer. In fact, just because it's the end of December and winter in Michigan, that probably wouldn't stop her from wanting to be outside. I'm going to have to put my foot down about that."

"Noted." Bill's grin said that he just might try it, but she was pretty sure he wouldn't.

She lifted her shoulders in a shrug. The businesswoman in her wanted to take charge.

Bill's grin said he knew it. He didn't seem to be intimidated by that part of her personality. Many men were. She was strong and smart and knew her mind, and it scared men.

Not Bill. He just let her bossiness roll over him while he went and did what he wanted to, unless she made sense to him, and then he wasn't afraid to do what she wanted.

This time, it was Bill who made sense.

She looked up, spinning around, looking at the sparkling stars dangling from the ceiling. "These are beautiful. Iva May's going to love them."

"Thanks. I hope so. I'm going to add some sparkle lights around the doorframes and maybe a couple of strips of some colored lights along the top of the walls. That should be enough to turn on at night, not just so whoever is helping her can see, but the light should make the stars sparkle and give her something to smile at if she wakes up."

They had made the schedule, with Bill and Kim and her all taking turns so that Iva May was never alone. Just in a few short days, she'd gone downhill to the point where she couldn't go up the stairs anymore. The hospital bed was coming just in time.

"That's smart. The lights should be dim enough for her to be able to sleep but bright enough for people to still be able to help her. Plus, it just makes the room more cheerful in the dark days of winter."

"That's what Kim and I thought. Did you get your business work done?" he asked, knowing that she had gone home after Iva May's appointment because she had some phone calls to make and an online meeting to attend. She was unwrapping herself from all the things that she had still been doing in business, which had been her plan all along, but it had been expedited because of Iva May's illness. She wanted to be here for her friend.

She supposed Bill had become as big a pull for her as Iva May.

She didn't want to admit that she looked forward to seeing him maybe even more than she looked forward to seeing Iva May, since it seemed like every day that she saw Iva May, she looked worse than she did the day before.

"The company should be here to deliver the bed at any time. I believe the portable toilet is also coming today." Bill said that matter-of-factly, and Bev tried to keep her face impassive although she cringed inside. Dying was not a fun thing.

Bill turned back toward the wall he'd been working on, stringing lights, and started to whistle.

"How can you be so happy?" she asked, the words coming out without her really thinking about them. They weren't nasty words, just baffled.

There was a lady dying—their friend, their mentor—in the next room, and he acted happy. It seemed wrong.

He stopped, his hands dropping, as he turned to face her.

"We've discussed this. Talk to Iva May. See what she says. I don't see any point in me being sad when she isn't. And she doesn't want us to be."

"But she's leaving us. That's a sad thing. I'm going to miss her."

The smile slowly slid off Bill's face, replaced by a look of compassion. "I think we're all going to miss her. And sadness is a natural feeling. It's okay for you to feel it. But it's also okay that some people might not want to dwell in their sadness. They might want to look at all the good things that are going to be happening."

"What could possibly be good?"

"Remember? Iva May is going to see her mom. Friends. Jesus. We'll have her memories. Lots of great memories. Maybe her death will teach us to appreciate our lives. The opportunities God gives us. And not take things for granted. There are always lessons. And while death is painful, we can learn from that. And we can be happy and joyful in the midst of it."

He made sense, but it just seemed odd to be happy while they watched someone die.

Was that negative thinking?

As a Christian, death was supposed to be just the beginning. A new beginning. Beautiful and happy and better than anything here on earth.

"Sometimes I think it's almost selfish for us to be sad. Especially if it makes the dying person feel guilty. Imagine that. Making someone feel guilty for dying, like they've chosen to." Bill's words were murmured, and he watched her closely.

He hadn't been shy about letting her know he was still interested in her. That alone had surprised her, since it was not in line with the Bill she knew, who was almost stoic, solid and quiet and wise.

He didn't go around blabbering about his feelings. But he had. For her.

And now, it seemed he was trying to teach her something. Not because he thought the way she was doing things was wrong, but clearly motivated because he thought there might be a better way. And he wanted to help her.

"I guess I just need to think about it," she finally said. His attention made her nervous. Especially when she knew how he felt. Even more so, because her traitorous heart wanted her to admit she felt the same way. She didn't want to. She wanted to be independent. And not ever do the marriage thing again.

"Take your time." Bill turned back around to the wall after giving her another searching look.

She didn't say anything more and didn't ask about his shop. He hadn't mentioned it while they were making the schedule, but as far as she knew, even through the winter, he kept it open. He could hardly be in his shop and still take care of Iva May.

She supposed if it were summer, it would be a bigger sacrifice, but still, there were ice fishermen, and the occasional tourist who came around, some to see the lights in the beachside town, and some locals.

This was supposed to be a season of rest, and instead of doing whatever it was that he enjoyed doing in the winter, he was here helping Iva May.

That's not something just any man would do.

She walked down the hall and into the living room where Iva May lay on the couch. Her eyes closed, her hands lying on top of her stomach, and the bottom half of her body covered with a blanket.

There was a small portable stand beside her with a glass of water and a Bible. Her phone lay on it too, and sweet piano hymns played softly.

A chair had been set up beside her, and Bev tiptoed over and sat down in it. She didn't want to wake Iva May.

Bill had said she'd been up until midnight, maybe she was tired.

But almost as though Iva May could feel her presence, Bev had no sooner settled in her seat than she opened her eyes.

"Bev." Her hand reached out, fumbling for Bev's. Bev took a hold of it and cradled it in her lap, hugging it between her two. Trying to warm the cold skin.

"Do you need another blanket?" She felt so cold.

Iva May shook her head from side to side, her brows furrowed a little as though she needed to think about that question. "No. I don't think so."

"I was just asking because your hand is cold."

Iva May gave a tired smile. "You are so warm."

Bev figured that was one way to look at it, it was her hands that were warm.

"Nice music," she said, unsure whether Iva May wanted to talk or not, even though her eyes were open and looking at Bev with so much love shining out from them that they made her uncomfortable almost. She felt like she didn't deserve love like that.

"It's something Bill said he thought I would enjoy. He was right. Angels' music."

"I bet the music's even better in heaven." Bev could feel her face smiling, and she wondered at that. Wasn't she supposed to be sad? Crying? But Bill was right, Iva May wasn't sad. She was happy. There was no regret on her face, nothing but happiness and love.

"I bet it is too," Iva May murmured. "Can I talk to you about Bill?"

Bev's eyes snapped back to Iva May's face. Normally, Iva May talked about whatever Bev brought up, respecting her silence on some subjects. Bill was normally one of the subjects Bev didn't talk about, although she always listened when Iva May talked about him.

"Sure." Her stomach tightened, and the hair on the back of her neck stood up. Maybe Iva May was going to tell her to leave Bill alone, that he'd been through enough and he didn't need the stress of another relationship.

"He loves you," Iva May said quietly.

Bev nodded slowly, then she looked from side to side to make sure there was no one else in the room, like someone might have walked in without her seeing them, before she leaned closer to Iva May and whispered, "I think I love him too."

"He promised me he would take care of you."

"That's what Bill does. He takes care of the people in this town. You know I'll be here permanently as soon as I get all of my business wrapped up in Detroit."

"No. I know he takes care of everyone in town, and he would take care of you just because you live here, but I mean...you're special."

Unsure what to say about that, Bev slowly stroked Iva May's hand and didn't say anything.

"I told him not to be afraid of his feelings. Not to be afraid to let you know. Because life is short."

So true. She couldn't believe she'd made it well into middle age, and she was looking pretty hard at being an older adult. In fact, she was considered a senior citizen by the state and could get that discount, if she had ever been brave enough to claim it, which she hadn't. She didn't want to be as old as what she was. She wanted to just keep living life and never face the end.

"I told him to be persistent." Iva May smiled a little, a conspiratorial smile. "I told him women like to be chased."

Despite herself, Bev chuckled. Even on her deathbed, Iva May was lifting people's spirits.

"I want to be the kind of woman that you are. Tell me. Tell me how I can be that way."

Iva May shook her head side to side on her pillow. "I'm talking about romance, and you're changing the subject."

"Bill deserves a better woman than me. He deserves someone like you."

"A dead woman?"

"You're not dead yet!"

"I'll be that way soon." She saw how Bev's eyes filled. "Don't cry for me. I'll be happier than I've ever been in just a bit. I can feel Jesus's peace in my soul, and I don't have a bit of fear."

"That's amazing. I wondered if you were afraid."

"I'm not. Not in the slightest. You're holding my hand physically, but last night, I could just feel the presence of God around me. I can't wait to go."

"That's why you're smiling and happy."

Iva May nodded. "But I want to see you happy too. Bill is a good man. And I know he's going to be trying to talk you into giving him a chance. I'd like you to tell me that you will."

"I'm too old."

"As long as you have a heartbeat, you're not too old."

"Then we're back to what I said before. Bill deserves someone so much better than me." Bev patted the hand that was slowly warming between hers. "Someone like you."

"But he loves you."

Bev looked down. She wanted Iva May to tell her the secret of how to be wise. How to be godly. How to be the kind of woman Iva May was. Sweet and humble and considerate. Always putting others first. Living a life of sacrifice, but making it seem like it was her privilege to do so, rather than letting everyone know how much she was giving up.

Iva May always could read her mind.

"Read your Bible. That's the secret. Reading, with the intention of letting God speak to you, letting Him show you the areas that you need to work on, and just submitting your life to Him."

"Submission. Sounds simple, but it's so hard," Bev said, not looking at Iva May. She'd tried submission. To God and to her husband, and it hadn't worked out for her. She was too headstrong.

"You don't fail and then quit. You fail, look at what you did wrong, make some adjustments to fix it, and then get up and try again. Day by day. Each day, you get a little better at it."

"Sounds simple, but I know from experience that even that is hard—day by day."

"Climbing a mountain is hard. And you do it step by step. Even when you fall down. Even when you slide back, even when you're tired. You just can't quit."

"I'm not a very good quitter. Sometimes I just don't have my head set to the right thing."

"That's where submission comes in. Allowing God to direct your life, rather than your own wants and desires."

"I was born with strong wants and desires. I want to manipulate everything around me."

"And God gave you strengths. For you to use."

"I need Jesus. To help me to know when I'm supposed to use them and when I'm supposed to just step back."

"See? You know what you need. Every hour, you need Jesus."

"And that's your secret?" A smile lifted the corners of her mouth as she met Iva May's eyes.

"I'm nothing without Jesus. That's the secret. I need him. Need the Bible. Need prayer. Never stop needing. Never think I'm enough without the Lord."

Iva May closed her eyes, and Bev worried that maybe she tired her out too much. So she just sat quietly, content to just be with her friend, but Iva May wasn't finished.

"You never promised me that you'd give Bill a chance."

Chapter 14

"Are you being a matchmaker on your deathbed?" Bev asked, not wanting to make that promise, not wanting to let her friend down.

"Bev. Life is short. Don't waste any more of it. And...your daughter needs parents."

She was talking about Kim. Bev hadn't talked to her much beyond working on the schedule, and talking about hospice, and talking about the things that Iva May would need.

Kim hadn't seemed to want to broach the parentage subject, and as far as she knew, she hadn't done it with Bill, either.

"Do you really think she's my daughter?" Bev asked, knowing she was already convinced in her own mind that she was, but she just wanted to hear it from Iva May.

Even though it didn't matter whether she was or she wasn't. She would be as much of a mother to Kim as Kim wanted her to be, but there was something inside her human body and soul that wanted to know whether Kim was a part of her and Bill or not.

Iva May nodded. "I didn't say this when I told you, maybe because it was hard enough to admit what I had done or at least allowed to happen. But my baby had a lot of hair on her head. Kim was almost bald. You know in hospitals they usually have hats on the babies' heads, and... I assumed you were young and probably were a little intimidated by the hospital staff, and maybe hadn't looked under your baby's hat. At least, you never said anything."

The light dawned in Bev's mind, because Iva May was right. It had been her first time in a hospital in any way, and the idea of touching her baby was a little intimidating. Like she needed permission or something. Definitely the idea of removing something that the hospital had put on was more than she would have done. She hadn't even considered it.

"I hadn't known."

"I honestly wasn't sure. I didn't have any pictures of her when she was just born, and I was a little groggy from the medication that they'd given me, but over the years, I'm almost positive that my baby had long hair. But the baby I took home from the hospital didn't."

Bev sat in silence. Whatever Iva May had done, or hadn't done, or allowed to happen, or whatever, had already been forgiven in her book. After all, God worked her life out in a miraculous way, and Kim had had an awesome mother.

There were no hard feelings. There was, maybe just a little, of what ifs? Would she and Bill still be together if they had had a baby between them? Would she have still believed the cheating accusations? Which in hindsight had been ridiculously stupid on her part. Since she knew the kind of character Bill had, even back then.

"Is Mom awake?" Kim's voice came from the entrance to the living room.

"I'm awake, honey," Iva May said, fatigue lining every syllable.

"You guys should see what Bill is doing to the kitchen. It looks amazing," Kim said, her hand on her stomach. "I feel like I should help him, but he told me to come in here and sit with Mom."

"I think that's a good idea." Bev stood, giving Kim her chair. "I'll go out and see if there's anything I can do to help."

Iva May's eyes cracked, and she gave Bev a smile that contained a lot of hope. Bev had the feeling that Iva May might be close to death, but she would be lying here praying that Bev and Bill were able to work out their differences.

Although at the age they were now, Bev didn't even think they really had differences, they were just too old for romance. Or had seen too much and didn't want to put the effort into something that wasn't as satisfying as what the world made it out to be.

Was she a cynic about love?

Yeah. She was pretty sure she was. And that wasn't really fair to Bill, and it wasn't fair to Iva May either.

She would go out, and she would talk to Bill. If he truly did love her, they had to be able to work something out.

"You have no right to keep me out of her room! I will go in and see her if I want to!"

The shrill voice came from the hall, with Bill's soft murmuring behind.

Bev and Kim gave each other a horrified look, then both of their gazes went to the doorway, where a woman, with her hair piled high on her head, a white cashmere shawl draped over her shoulders, skinny pants tucked into high-heeled leather boots, appeared in the doorway.

"Iva May! I do declare, you should have told me you weren't feeling well. You know I would run to help you any way I could," the woman said, her hand going to her chest, as she walked in the room, her expression looking sincere.

Bev thought she recognized the woman as Tricia, Iva May's husband's sister.

"Tricia," Iva May said weakly, no indication on her face that she was not happy to see this woman who hadn't talked to her for thirty years if Bev recalled the story correctly.

"Iva May! I knew you would be happy to see me," she said, giving Bill a glare.

"Of course. You traveled a long distance to come. Of course you're welcome."

"That's exactly what I thought," the woman said, stopping at Kim's chair. "Darling, if you'll excuse me, I need to sit down. I can't stand as long as I used to."

Kim's eyebrows went up, but she said, "Of course, Aunt Tricia." Kim stood up and gave her the chair she'd been sitting in. "Can I get you anything, Mom?"

"I'll be fine for a few minutes. And then I'm going to need to take a rest. I'll talk to Tricia just for a bit."

Bev took that to mean they should come back in ten minutes or so and see if they could get the woman to go.

All of them filed out of the room as Tricia leaned back and crossed her legs.

"Oh, Kimmy dear, would you mind grabbing me a glass of juice from the refrigerator? Preferably cranberry, if you have it." Her tone said everyone should have cranberry juice.

"I'll see what I can do, Aunt Tricia," Kim said, just a touch of irritation leaking into her tone.

Bev had to say she was impressed at Kim's ability to be kind. Although, being that she was Iva May's daughter, not only had she been taught kindness, but she'd been shown a great example of kindness.

No one said anything until they were standing in the kitchen together.

"I want to be like Iva May when I grow up," Bev said.

Bill grinned, and then one of his big hands came down and landed on her shoulder. "I think you're more like her than you realize."

"That's true, Bev," Kim said as she opened the refrigerator door and bent over, looking to see what they had for juice. "Mom always said you were like a daughter to her. Even though you're only fifteen years younger."

"That's all the younger you are than Bev," Bill pointed out reasonably. And Bev kinda thought that he said it as though the idea of Kim being Bev's daughter was an established fact.

Kim didn't seem bothered by that but grabbed a container and pulled it out. Turning, she said, "That's true. Although fifteen is rather young to be a mom."

"It sure is," Bev said, fervently almost. She hadn't felt prepared, not in the slightest, to be a mom. Of course, being a mom was a little bit of an overwhelming responsibility, and she wasn't sure anyone was ever prepared to be a mom. Not like they needed to be.

"I hope orange juice is okay with Aunt Tricia." Kim set the container down on the counter, since there was no table anymore, and opened the cupboard door to grab a glass.

"It looks so different in here without the table," she said as she reached out, pulling one down.

"There's supposed to be a hospital bed here by the end of the day. That'll really make it look different."

"The stars do it for me." Bev looked up at the glittering shapes hanging from the ceiling. "I think this would be beautiful to lie and look at. It was nice of you to do it."

Bill jerked his head but didn't say anything.

Kim had finished pouring the orange juice and put the container back in the refrigerator. She came to the counter and picked up the glass. "I feel like I should have this on a golden serving tray or something."

"Do you want me to take it in?" Bill offered.

"No. If Mom can be nice to her, I can too."

Bill nodded, and Kim left.

"I'm not sure what it is about someone dying that brings out the worst in some people. I haven't seen Iva May's sister-in-law here since before my marriage broke up."

Bev sighed. "Iva May was so gracious. I was just asking her to tell me how she became like she is."

"I'm sure she said it was all the Lord. She's humble."

"You're right. She also told me that...that she wanted to see us together." Bev swallowed. She'd always been direct. She'd never been any good at acting any other way.

Bill stilled in the act of folding up the stepladder that he'd used to hang the stars. "Don't feel like you have to just because it's the wish of a dying woman. I want to honor her as much as I can, but she's not gonna determine the way our lives go, if it's not the way the Lord wants them to go. Plus, I'd hate to think that you're with me just because she told you she wanted us to be together and not because you wanted to be."

Bev used her fingernail to run along the edge of the counter. She didn't look up. "I don't know what I want. I told her..." Could she say it? She took a breath. "I told her I loved you. It's true. But it's also true that I don't want to do the marriage thing again. I don't want to get stuck in something I can't get out of. I want to be free."

"Yeah. I totally get that. I had my last wife in the dungeon in the basement. I'd put you there too. I fed her once a week, whether she needed it or not, and took her for a walk on Valentine's Day."

Bev laughed. Bill smiled, but there was a little hurt in his eyes.

"I didn't mean to say that you're a mean, angry tyrant, one who would never allow me to be what I want to be."

"Really?"

She crossed her arms over her chest and leaned against the counter. "Really. I know you're different than most, if not all, of the other men I know. But...there is still this part of me that's scared."

"I guess there's a part of me that's scared, but for different reasons. I... I don't usually announce to people how I feel about them. And that's made me a little uncomfortable, wondering how you felt too."

"Well, now you know. I love you. I never stopped."

"But we aren't going to do anything about it?"

She shrugged her shoulders and turned away. "I honestly don't know."

"Would you be interested in going on a date? We don't have to wait until Saturday night. In fact, I think for old people, we can go on a date anytime we want to. Tonight. Tomorrow."

"Can we date while Iva May is dying?"

"Why not? She wants us to. And Kim will take the evening shift. I wasn't planning on leaving her here by herself all the time, but she's forty years old. She can handle being alone while I romance you."

"You've never been very romantic. I'm pretty sure nothing has changed in that area."

"Maybe I'm trying to be a better man. Maybe you're not the only one who might be looking at being over the hill but still thinking that there are improvements that could be made."

"I think you're pretty much perfect. I don't really think you have to worry about improvements."

Raised voices drew their attention, and their eyes met, widening, before Bill turned and moved toward the hallway, walking at about twice his normal speed.

"I will be here as much as I want to be here. After all, Iva May and I were related and good friends before you were even born." Tricia held the orange juice in her hand, waving it around as she spoke. "Tell her, Iva May. I have as much right to be here as anyone and even more than that person right there." Her eyes landed squarely on Bev. "And that man behind her. He's no relation to you at all. Neither of them is. I will take a turn taking care of you."

Bev had a feeling if Tricia were taking care of Iva May, she might end up smothering her with a pillow rather than helping her, but she bit her tongue so those words didn't escape and tried to shove the thought out of her head. It wasn't kind.

"Tricia." Iva May's voice was sharper and louder than it had been for over a week. "These people are my family. All of them. And they are my friends. My very good friends, whom I talk to every day. You are welcome to visit, but you are not welcome to insult them in my house. If you feel the need to do so, you may show yourself out."

"Well, I might just have to do that," Tricia said, standing, setting the juice down on the small, portable table. "I don't want to be where I am no longer welcome. I thought we were friends, but obviously..." She paused for effect. "I was wrong." She emphasized each word before she slipped out of the room.

"I will be back, and I will expect that you all will have come to your senses and will give me my proper place and the respect that is my due."

Chapter 15

B ill walked up the front walk of Bev's house and rang the doorbell, nervously clutching the small gift he had brought in his hands and trying to still the F5 tornado in his stomach.

His throat was too dry to swallow, and his hands felt sweaty despite the below freezing temperatures.

He didn't have time to stand and second-guess himself about the gift, because the door opened almost immediately.

"Come on in. It's freezing out."

"Literally," Bill murmured as he walked in, closing the door behind him.

When Bev had agreed to go out on a date with him, he considered it a win. But then he had so much jumbled up in his mind, trying to figure out what Pastor Kane had been telling him, what he needed to do, what he should focus on in order to change the direction of his life.

He didn't want to keep making the same mistakes over and over again.

The changing, being uncomfortable, was hard.

"I just need to grab my coat and put my boots on," Bev said, moving away, not like he was going to greet her with a kiss anyway. That would be way too premature. He hadn't even been sure she'd agree to go out with him, let alone allow him to kiss her.

"I brought this for you." He held up the gift bag in his hand, hoping she couldn't see his hands were trembling.

"You brought me a gift?" She turned, her head tilted, her hand going to her heart like she couldn't believe it.

"It's just something small."

The way she acted, she wasn't used to receiving gifts, which surprised him. But maybe people looked at her, saw how much money she had, and thought there was nothing they could get her that she couldn't buy herself.

But while Pastor Kane hadn't explicitly said this, Bill kind of thought that maybe it wasn't the gift itself but the thoughtfulness behind it that might mean something to her.

She peeled back the paper. Her hair, no longer sun-bleached blonde but more of a sandy blonde streaked with strands of gray, shone in the overhead light.

The face of the young girl was still there, but the skin wasn't as smooth, with more spots of color, more wrinkles, more wisdom.

If he had to choose between the older version of Bev and the younger version, it would be an easy choice. He wanted her the way she was now. Her age and experience matched his.

"I can't believe you remembered," Bev whispered in a shocked tone as she pulled the small figurine of a basset hound out of the bag.

He wasn't sure how she thought he could forget. And then he remembered that maybe she needed to hear the words, so he said, "I've had two of those since you moved away from Blueberry Beach. I bought them together. I still have the other one at home."

He couldn't quite get to the feelings part of that, but hopefully she could understand what it meant.

"We always talked about having two basset hounds and four children in our cottage by the sea." She looked up at him. Her eyes shone, he realized with fear. Was she going to cry? He hadn't meant to make her cry.

His heart, already beating hard and fast, tripled its tempo. What would he do if she cried? "I think maybe we won't have the children, but the basset hounds are still a possibility."

She bit her lip. He wasn't sure if it was his reference to children or his reference to the possibility of them having a relationship. "Thank you. This is beautiful, and I'll put it on the mantle. I definitely love the idea that you remembered. That really means something to me." She cut off abruptly, turning and walking to the mantle, and setting the figurine carefully among some greenery.

She appreciated him remembering? He supposed paying attention to what she said and remembering it showed caring. At least to her. He tried to keep that in mind, because there were a lot of things to remember, but more than that, paying attention to her now and remembering what she said was probably just as important.

Maybe with his first wife, he had a tendency to be absentminded and not consider that what she was saying was anything he really wanted to listen to.

Whether he had wanted to or not, it showed consideration and caring for him to do so.

That was one mistake he could keep from making again. Hopefully.

She turned around, smoothing her hands down her pants and looking much more nervous and far less cool than she had when she'd opened the door.

He thought that was probably a good thing.

"I wasn't sure where you were taking me, so I hope I'm dressed all right?"

He spent a lot of time thinking about this too, since he hadn't been on a date in over a decade. And before that, it wasn't like he dated a lot.

"You look fine. I wasn't going anywhere fancy, if that's your fear."

"I guess. Or, I don't know. If we're going somewhere warm, I'm a little overdressed."

"I was going to take you to Simone's Subs. I thought we'd grab them to go and go up to Strawberry Sands and the overlook to eat them. We might be able to make it in time to watch the sun go down."

Her brows had shot up as he had spoken, and then she smiled, and he felt like it was another win.

"I haven't been to Simone's in decades. Is it still open?"

He nodded. "I don't go there much. It's not the same without you, but she's still there."

She smiled, and it warmed his chest. Because while it was happy, it almost looked like a sappy smile. One where she couldn't believe what he'd done and appreciated it.

Simone's mother was a Blueberry Beach native who had started the sub shop and named it after her only daughter. Not long after Simone graduated, she had taken over the sub shop. It wasn't a particularly fancy place, but the food was good, and it held many happy memories for Bev.

Doing that exact thing, picking up subs at Simone's and going up to Strawberry Sands to sit at the overlook had been one of the main things they'd done on their "dates" when they'd been together but hadn't wanted anyone to know about them all those years ago.

She finished putting her coat on in silence, and although he was tempted to step forward and help her, he kept his hands at his sides. He did want to touch her, wanted to have his arm around her, wanted to be close, to kiss her. But he didn't want that to be all their relationship was.

Even back when they'd been together before, they did a lot of laughing and joking and having fun together. But he hadn't been able to resist a physical relationship when she had almost pushed for it.

Maybe one of his biggest regrets.

Grabbing her purse, she came over and stood in front of him. "I'm ready. I'm sorry you're probably not used to someone taking so long."

"I seem to remember there are distinct differences between the way men get ready and the way women get ready. And that's okay. I kinda like it that we're different."

She gave him a look that said maybe he'd said everything right. For once. He opened the door.

He took her arm, just a gentle grip, as they walked down the steps and down the walk to his car. There was no ice on the walk, but snow blew on both sides, and he wanted an excuse to touch her.

If he were being honest.

Taking her around, he opened her door, and she gave him a look before she got in. He thought it was a good look, maybe because he opened her door, or maybe because she was just happy to be with him. He wasn't sure.

It took him a little bit, because he wasn't much of a talker, but he finally loosened up enough to start a conversation about the weather, and the changes in Blueberry Beach over the decades, and the fact that he hadn't been to Strawberry Sands in years.

Bev had always been easy to talk to, and beyond their awkward interactions of the past, they settled back into their easy communication.

The topics were light as they stopped in at Simone's and chatted for a bit. If she was surprised to see them together, she didn't say so, although she did look between them a few times, almost as though she was trying to remember why they seemed familiar.

Regardless, they got their subs and drinks and were back on the road, heading north to Strawberry Sands and the bluffs, continuing their easy companionship. It almost made a man forget the decades that had passed and feel young again, when he had a beautiful woman beside him who acted like she thought he was funny and smart and fun to be around.

The nice thing about the bluffs was they could pull right into the parking lot and be very close to the edge, looking out over Lake Michigan, with a beautiful view of the lake and the setting sun.

For summer days, when it was warm, there was a trail people could walk down that would take them right to the edge of the bluffs. They had often gone down and sat on the edge. They'd never jumped off, like other kids had, but it was a beautiful view, calming and peaceful, and even once the sun went down and the stars came out, he couldn't think of anything that compared.

Those had been some of the best nights of his life, sitting on the bluffs with Bev, just holding her hand and talking.

Life hadn't been simple, exactly, but he'd been with the one who fit him, made him better and understood him, and when Bev looked at him, it was like she only saw his good.

He hoped he'd been the same for her.

"I guess we could walk down the trail if you want to, but even as a young adult, I think it would have been too cold."

Bev pulled the bag of subs up and shook her head. "I'm happy here in the warm car. The view is just as good, and the company is perfect."

She handed him his sub, and their fingers brushed as he took it. Her eyes flickered, and he wondered if that was because she felt the same charge that he had when their skin met.

Crazy for an old man.

He prayed over their food, and they started to eat in silence.

"I'd forgotten how good these things are," Bev finally said. "I can't believe I haven't had one in forty years."

"Wow. What a waste of a life," Bill said, meaning it as a joke, but Bev didn't laugh.

"I was just kidding," he said.

"I know. But I've actually been thinking that for a while. What have I actually done with my life? Has it been wasted?"

"You built a successful business. It's not wasted." He cleared his throat, wanting to say this just right, because he didn't want to say anything else that she took more seriously than he intended. Or not the right way. "You talk like your life is over. It's not. You have plenty of life left in front of you. It's not like there's nothing that you can do now, nothing you can change. Nothing you can start."

Maybe it was obvious what he was angling for—for her to start a relationship with him—but he didn't really care. That was part of what he wanted to convince her of, no doubt. That it wasn't too late for them.

"I'm fifty-five. Just saying that makes me feel old. I never thought I would be *fifty-five*. I absolutely never thought I'd be alone, unmarried, with no family to speak of, and moving back to my hometown at this age. It feels...like I've just gone right back to where I started and haven't accomplished anything."

"You don't know how much life is left in front of you. There's plenty of time to accomplish whatever you want to. Not that what you've done already doesn't count."

"Maybe you didn't hear me say I'm fifty-five? Almost at retirement age. The state considers me a senior citizen." Her voice held humor but also exasperation. Like being a senior citizen was the last thing she wanted.

"So you're just going to throw in the towel?"

"I guess I'm saying I don't really see a point in starting a relationship. There's no time left for one. I'll never have a golden wedding anniversary. We'll never have kids or grandkids together. We have completely separate lives. You have jokes that I won't get, because you've experienced things that I didn't. We just...can't spend our lives together and have that foundation that people are supposed to have when they're our age."

Bill had never considered any of that, but she was right. People who got married in their twenties, or even in their thirties, had a shot at being together fifty years, which was a lot of time and something worth celebrating. They had history. Shared experiences. Time spent together raising a family and getting to know each other. They'd have mutual friends and mutual people they'd both rather avoid. So much rich history that would make for beautiful memories and bind them more strongly together.

"I guess that applies even more to me, since I'm older than you are."

"I don't mean it as an insult. But I just don't see any point in starting something. Look at Iva May. She's only seventy, and she's leaving us. That will be me in just fifteen years. It hardly seems worth it."

"That's funny, because when you're twenty, you don't think, *I'm not going to start this because I might die in a car accident tomorrow.* You don't think about the rest of your life, you just see what God has put in front of you, and you put your hand to it and do it. And if He takes you early, then He takes you. I'm not sure that just because of our age, we should think any differently."

"We should definitely be thinking with an eye toward the future."

"But we're not guaranteed a future. Not one at twenty, not when we're our age. All we're guaranteed is today, and we're supposed to make the best of it."

Maybe her words made him a little angry. Because he didn't want to just give up and say he was too old. Sure, maybe his age would keep them from doing some things, and yeah, maybe there were things they'd missed out on—kids and family and shared memories and golden anniversaries—but that was no reason not to start. He wasn't going to live the rest of his life focused on what he didn't have, what he'd missed, what he was missing. How sad.

He wanted to live until it was time to die; he didn't want to just get ready to die and throw up his hands and walk away from everything that he could accomplish, and he felt like there were a lot of things to do. Even if he was just a shop owner in a sleepy little lakeside town.

"Maybe it's because I haven't lived your life, haven't been at the height of success, haven't started a company, a successful multimillion-dollar international company, and seen everything that you have. I've just been in my place, day by day, living in Blueberry Beach."

"Doing everything you can to help everyone you can. There's a lot more satisfaction in that at the end of a life than there is in chasing after material things, which is what I feel like I've done my whole life. Like climbing to the top of the ladder was somehow more important than the people around me. My success came before everything."

"I don't believe that for one second. You talk about yourself like you were ruthless and cutthroat, and I know for a fact that's not true."

She blew out a breath, studying her half-eaten sub. "No. I never did anything immoral. And I tried not to be unkind, but...my decisions were made based on me and what was best for me. And my idea of best for me was making money and being successful in business."

Suddenly the light came on in his head, and he thought he understood what she was saying.

Chapter 16

B ill lifted a brow. "You regret not being here more with Iva May, now that she's leaving."

"I do." Bev's head turned, and her eyes grew big, surprised that he seemed to have figured out what her issue was.

"I've definitely run over in my mind what I could have done differently. I think there are a lot of things. Things I would change if I could. I do think we can learn from that. We can learn that if we don't want to live our lives full of regrets, we have to make the right decisions in real time. Even when they're hard. But I also think that it's dangerous to dwell in the past. Because we start to feel hopeless, and we get down on ourselves, and I don't see any benefit."

"Maybe that's what's happening with me."

"Maybe, because the idea that there's no point in starting anything new at our age is a dangerous one. You're basically saying we might as well roll over and die."

"Plenty of people retire and do nothing and are happy in retirement."

"I guess that's probably not going to be me. I'm always going to want to start new things, to work on the things that I have, to do what I can to be a blessing to the people around me. Isn't that the purpose of our lives? Bring glory to God? God doesn't have a retirement age listed in the Bible. We just keep working until we die."

"Like Moses led the people of Israel until God decided it was time for him to move on, and he died on Mount Pisgah."

"Exactly. Moses didn't quit doing what he was called to do, he didn't quit moving forward just because he knew he was getting old."

"Maybe there's more to it than that," Bev said softly.

Bill paused with his hoagie halfway to his mouth. More? He wasn't sure what more there could be. But he wasn't going to let that go. Pastor Kane's words about caring, and not just saying that he cared and was interested, but showing it, came to mind, and he pried, when maybe he wouldn't have before. "What do you mean, more?"

She set her lips and stared out the windshield at the remnants of the sunset, and he thought maybe he pried too much. That was why he didn't ask probing questions. Because it made other people uncomfortable, not to mention him, and it opened up the possibility of rejection.

Finally, she settled her sub on the paper on her lap and spoke.

"It's scary. It's one thing, I would think, to grow old with someone. From your youth to your old age. You've been with them, have walked side by side with them, they've seen the battles that you've fought, you fought some together. They understand your scars and why you are the way you are."

"I don't want to minimize what you're saying, because I get it, but we've already figured out that that's not our life. It's never going to happen for us. So there's no point in wishing for it or getting upset because you don't have it. You have to love what you've got. It's the life that God has given you; it's the one that you're to use for Him."

"I'm sorry. I guess I wasn't being clear. It's not that I necessarily regret that, because you're right. I can't change the past. It is what it is. But I was saying for moving on, for relationships in particular, not necessarily starting anything new, but a relationship. A new person isn't going to understand your scars. They're not gonna look at the signs of old age and know how they got there. They're not going to...appreciate the battles you've had. Because they weren't there. And yes, I get that we can't choose that, but it's just something that I'm a little...afraid of." She turned her head and met his eyes when she said that. He felt like it was a confession that she was allowing him to hear.

He jerked his head up just a little but didn't say anything. What was there to say?

"Do you see this?" she asked, pointing to her face.

"It's beautiful," he said simply, honestly. It wasn't youthful like it was forty years ago, but it was Bev now, and he would always think she was beautiful.

She grunted. "It's not. It's old. It's wrinkled. It's lost its youthful glow and elasticity. Makeup doesn't even make it look good anymore," she said with humor in her voice.

He opened his mouth to argue. To tell her that she didn't need makeup. And that outward beauty didn't matter anyway, but she kept talking and he closed his mouth.

"The rest of my body is the same. I couldn't possibly strut around in a bikini anymore. I don't even want to wear shorts. Wrinkles and dark spots and scars and stretch marks." She gave him a side glance. "Cellulite. Rolls where there didn't used to be rolls and everything droops."

She took a breath, as though she didn't really want to keep talking, but she wanted him to understand. "Getting married means getting naked. I don't want to be naked in front of anyone, especially not someone I...love and who I care about what he thinks. What I was saying was maybe if I had grown old with someone, it wouldn't be that big of a deal, but now? To have someone come in and see my body, I can't even begin to imagine. The very thought almost makes me shake with fear."

Bill grunted, giving her one last glance, before his own sub landed in his lap, and his head leaned back against the seat as he looked out at the skyline of Lake Michigan, unseeing.

He hadn't even considered that. Although, he supposed in the back of his mind, he knew that intimacy at their age would be different than intimacy forty years ago. But he'd figured they'd figure it out. People had been doing it for thousands of years.

"Isn't that part of what joining our lives together is? I mean, I'm not looking for a twenty-year-old with a twenty-year-old's body and a twenty-year-old's view of life. I've been there, I've done that, I'm smarter than that now, and I want someone with the same kind of wisdom that

I have. And that kind of wisdom, that kind of knowledge, that kind of experience, comes with a different physical appearance. Anyhow, I guess you don't see too many pinups of fifty- or sixty-year-olds, and maybe I wouldn't look at those anyway, so I don't know what a fifty-five-year-old body looks like." He felt a little odd saying that. Like he was getting personal by talking about her body, and that really wasn't what he wanted from their relationship right now, but it was a fear she had that was keeping her from moving forward with him. So he felt like he needed to say it.

"But I don't care. It doesn't matter to me. I'm not looking for physical perfection. After all," he patted his own protruding stomach and then ran a hand over his balding hair, "I'm pretty far from perfect. I look a lot different than I did when I was twenty. As I recall, I looked more like a beanpole than Santa Claus. Now, I've got the Santa Claus thing going. I suppose I could have the Santa Claus beard and let it grow longer, but up here," he patted the top of his head, "I'm looking more in common with a bowling ball than I do with my twenty-year-old self. It never occurred to me that might be an issue. Will those things bother you?"

"Of course not." She wrinkled her nose up and acted like him asking her almost offended her.

"Then what in the world would make you think that I care?"

"Because men are different than women. It wasn't your body I was attracted to to begin with back in the day."

"Um, be careful about that. Because as I recall, I was pretty proud of it." He grinned at her, and she chuckled a little. Maybe he should have kept the humor out of the conversation, but it felt like it was getting heavy, more heavy than what he wanted to be, although he tried to recall that maybe women liked those heavy, intimate conversations, where they mostly made him uncomfortable.

"Seriously. I know women have that reputation, but men, at least the men that I know, are sensitive about, maybe not their face, but their

physique. Their height." Bill grinned a little. "It seems like men are always supposed to be six feet tall with broad shoulders and long legs
and lots of muscles, and that's never been me. I admit to being sensitive about it. Back when I was younger, I was too skinny to have defined
muscles, and now, I'm just plain fat. And bald, which is another sore
spot. Plus I'm short. So, if we're chalking up all of our flaws, I think I've
got you beat."

"You're not short. You're taller than me."

"But I'm not *manly* tall."

It didn't really bother him anymore. Not much, but particularly in
high school, and the decade after, it had been a hard pill to swallow to
know that he wasn't going to be any taller than what he was. Not just
for his own sense, but particularly for women, since they always seemed
to go after the tall men. And he was average, or slightly less than average
in height, and didn't stick out at all. Not physically.

"I don't care how tall you are." She lifted her shoulder. "Okay. I kinda like that you're taller than me. Does that make me shallow?"

"I think it does," he said, lifting a shoulder a little and smiling to let
her know he was teasing her.

"But the muscles and this..." She tapped her own stomach, which
was not nearly as slender as it was when she was a teen. "Your hair,
none of it matters. Because of the character you have. Your compassion.
Your loyalty. I know you're going to be honest. When you say that stuff
doesn't matter, I know you're not just giving me a line or trying to say
what you think I want to hear."

"Well, don't give me too much credit, because I've been trying to
say what I've been thinking or at least trying to form thoughts into
words because I think that's what you want to hear."

"But you're not making stuff up, dishing out compliments because
you want to get somewhere with me. There's a difference." Bev lifted her
brows and looked at him, waiting for him to agree.

"Right. I'm not lying. I'm just...talking when normally maybe I wouldn't. About stuff that I normally wouldn't."

"Exactly." Her face didn't look nearly as heavy as it had when they started their conversation, and he felt like maybe they were getting somewhere because she understood that just as she had insecurities about the way she looked, he did as well, but he wasn't going to let them stop him. He hoped she came to that same decision.

"Just, women seem to be judged a lot more on how they look. There's a standard for us. There is a certain way men expect us to look. We're supposed to be slender. We're not supposed to have wrinkles, no varicose veins, white hair, or stretch marks, or, God forbid, cellulite."

"When you're talking about men 'in general,' you can leave me out of that, because, like I said, I hadn't really thought of it before, but I don't really care about any of it. I mean, I guess I like that you're active, that we can do things together, but that kind of makes you who you are. I'm not sure I would be as attracted to you if you were content to lie on the couch all day and watch TV."

"I would be a completely different person if I did that."

"Yeah. That's what I was saying. You'd probably be a different size, but it wouldn't be your size that caused my disinterest. It would be your activities that led to it. Does that make sense?"

"Yeah. I feel the same. Although after seeing what I've seen all my life, and while I can easily say that it's not the way you look that's attractive to me, I do like this." She ran her hand over her cheek, indicating his stubble.

He smiled. "I remember that from when you were a teen. I didn't have much, but you'd mentioned it a time or two, and I suppose all my life I've remembered and had it, just because of the things you said when we were together."

"You have stubble because I said I liked it back when I was fifteen?" she said, disbelief dripping from every word.

"Yeah. Basically. Sorry if that makes me shallow."

She laughed at that. "It doesn't make you shallow. I just...didn't know. It kind of makes me feel good. Like you cared about what I wanted. What I said. What I liked."

"I did. I do. I always will."

"Well," she said, turning back and looking out the windshield like what she was about to say wasn't something she wanted to meet his gaze over. "Maybe that's part of what I'm afraid of, because I remember what you liked, and it was the indent of my waist, and the flare of my hips, and—"

"I'm not going to deny that I liked all of them. And you could go on, because there was a lot more of your body that I liked, but from the perspective of a sixty-year-old versus a twenty-year-old, I can tell you it was the least important part."

She looked over at him slowly. And said softly, "Really?"

He nodded. "I guarantee it. You talked about character being important, and that's true for me too. I know your determination. I know your willingness to work hard. I know your love for Iva May and the generosity you've shown to the town of Blueberry Beach. I probably don't even know everything you've done there, either, because you've been humble and quiet about your giving. I know your smile, and your good attitude, and your desire to make things beautiful. I love all that. Whatever package it comes in."

Maybe they were the right words, and he had a feeling they were, because she gave him a relieved look, then picked up her sub and took a bite.

Chapter 17

Bev waited for Bill to come around the side of his truck to open her door.

She couldn't keep the smile off of her face, nor did she want to. This had been the best evening she'd had in a really long time. And they hadn't even done anything. Just sat and talked, ate together, looked at a beautiful sunset, and had the kind of conversation that made her feel like they really understood each other.

"What are you smiling about?" Bill asked as he opened her door, a smile on his own face.

"The same thing you are, probably," she said, stepping out.

"I doubt it. I'm smiling because I'm with a beautiful woman, who also happens to be intelligent and funny and compassionate and kind. And I had a good time with her."

His words filled her heart with warmth, and when their arms brushed, and his fingers closed around hers, it felt like the most natural thing in the world. Even though it also felt strange. Because it was Bill, and it had been so long.

"Well, my smile is for the same thing, only it's because I just had a really great evening with a man who's rock solid, and who has character, and who doesn't seem to mind all of my flaws or even see them."

"What flaws?" Bill asked around his grin.

"Exactly. But I think more than that, I appreciate your conversation. It wasn't just surface stuff about how pretty the sunset was or how the town has changed, although we did talk about those things, but you made the effort to talk about deeper stuff, things that I care about, and you seemed to care about how I felt and what I thought."

"There is no 'seemed to' about it. I do care."

"Tonight I felt that caring. I felt like you were interested in me and what I said and how I felt. Like you weren't just asking to get brownie points."

"I'm not very good at getting brownie points."

"I know. You're not very good at just saying things. You always mean them. There's substance behind your words. They're not just empty flattery or catering to what you think I want."

Bill was quiet as he walked slowly beside her, up her walk, stopping at her door. He seemed to be thinking about what she had said, and she loved that. Like the things that she said he didn't just pay attention to, but he chewed on them and responded to them.

So many times, she'd been out with men who asked questions and then didn't seem to pay attention to the answer, were just more interested in talking about themselves or in asking her the questions that they knew women wanted to hear but had no interest in her answer, just wanting to get somewhere with her or being polite in a surface kind of way.

Bill had been different. Bill had always been different.

"Pastor Kane said I needed to not be afraid to open up a little, take some risks. He also pointed out some areas where I haven't been very good over the years and where I could improve." He looked down at the ground, almost as though he were embarrassed. "I've been trying."

Bill had never been emotional. That was part of what she loved about him. That he was rock solid and didn't get tossed and turned by every little piece of drama that happened in the world. That he knew what he believed and had a solid anchor. But tonight, he hadn't been afraid to dig a little deeper, engage with her in the kind of emotional things she appreciated and that made her feel closer to him. She felt like she got a little glimpse of him and that he'd been interested in the little glimpse of herself that she'd exposed.

"It was your interest tonight that made me feel special," she finally said.

"I want to know everything about you. What you think, how you think, what you want, your hopes and dreams, because I want them to work with mine."

Maybe he was being a little *too* open and emotional for her. Maybe she wasn't ready to hear that because it scared her a little. She wasn't ready to give all of herself like that.

Even if she thought that though, she knew if Bill and she didn't end up together, her secrets were safe with him. The things that were precious to her would be precious to him, and anything she said, anything she did, wouldn't go any further than the two of them, unless it was okay with her. No matter how angry he got at her, no matter how far apart they drifted eventually, she was sure about those things. Because that was the kind of man Bill was.

"I feel safe telling you those things." She looked him square in the eye, waited for him to look at her. "And I want to know those things about you." Her words were sincere, reflecting her heart.

Back when they dated before, she pushed for physical intimacy. Bill had been reluctant. Although he'd believed her when she said she was eighteen, he wanted to wait until her graduation and get married.

She, on the other hand, knew her graduation wasn't happening for years, and she hadn't been totally sure she wanted to graduate and get married right away anyway.

At any rate, she'd always been the one to make the moves.

As she stared at him now, she kept telling herself she'd be patient and let him decide how fast they were going to move.

It was like her turning over a new leaf since she was used to being the one in charge.

Bill's way would have been better, if she would have listened back then. So it made sense for her to wait now.

But as the silence stretched between them, and the cold air swirled around, she couldn't stop her impatience. Why didn't he move? Why didn't he lean closer and at least kiss her good night?

She could ask him in, but she was almost certain he would say no. Finally, she figured she had a choice between that and one other thing, and she chose the second.

"I've been hoping for the last two hours that you were going to kiss me good night, but I've been telling myself I'd wait for you to make any moves. I'm trying to keep my word to myself, but I'm a little impatient."

She wrung her hands together in front of her, not something a fifty-five-year-old lady should be doing. Surely she should have outgrown it by now.

Apparently not, since she couldn't get them to stop while Bill stared at her, his mouth partially open, his face in shadow, so she couldn't see his expression.

"I think you're serious," he finally said.

"I am. I know I'm used to being in charge, and I'm used to making decisions and forging ahead—"

"You want to kiss me. That's what I'm talking about."

Her mouth clamped shut. Why did that surprise him?

So all her good plans flew out the window, because she didn't want him doubting for one second whether or not she wanted to, didn't want him thinking she hadn't already because of anything other than wanting to wait on him.

She pulled her hands apart and stepped closer so they were touching, then wrapped her arms around his shoulders, lifting her head up and standing on her tiptoes.

He'd said to her tonight about how he wished he were taller, and so she couldn't help but murmur just before her lips touched his, "You're the perfect height. If you were any taller, I'd need a stepladder, and I don't want to wait while I go find one."

So they were both smiling as their mouths met, and her eyes closed and Bill's arms wrapped around her, pulling her even tighter.

It had been forty years since she kissed him, and she didn't know whether she'd expected it to feel familiar or not, but Bill wasn't anything like the kid he'd been, and neither was she.

While she believed what they had way back was something solid that could have lasted for a lifetime, it still felt hot and more like a meteor flashing across the sky than what she felt at this very moment. While there was still passion in his kiss, and enough emotion to make her heart beat fast in her throat and her stomach clench tightly, it also felt patient, unhurried, and somehow deeper. More thorough. Like he was less concerned about getting to the end and more concerned about enjoying it and making it last.

When he finally lifted his head, both of them were breathing unsteadily, but they were both smiling as well.

"You got better at that over the years."

"I can't imagine how, no one can kiss like you."

"I'm pretty sure that was all you. After all, you made the first move."

Her mouth opened, and she gasped in mock outrage. "Are you making fun of me?"

"I don't think too many people are brave enough to do that, are they?"

He was. He was teasing her, and she loved it. Because he was right, in her work, she was usually on top, and people didn't mess with the boss. She loved that he wasn't afraid of her. Although he absolutely respected her, he still wasn't afraid to have some laughs at her expense, as long as she was laughing too.

"I admire your bravery," she said cheekily.

"I was kind of admiring it too."

They laughed together, and then he sobered. "Seriously, I've always loved that part of being with you, but that wasn't all I loved, not now, and not before, either."

"I know. That's what makes you different."

He stared at her intently for a bit, then seemed to shake himself. "You go on in, and I'll wait until I'm sure you're okay."

"Do you...do you want to come in?"

"I do. But I'm not going to."

That's what she figured he would say. Although, she wasn't sure he would have admitted that he wanted to come in to begin with.

She nodded, knowing it was for the best.

"I would take another kiss before you go in," his voice said next to her ear as she turned to open her door.

He didn't have to ask twice. She turned back around, and it was a long time before she walked into her house.

Chapter 18

Bev opened the door to Iva May's house and slipped in quietly. She had been unable to sleep after coming home with Bill, so eventually she texted Kim and asked if it was okay if she came over and sat with Iva May for a while.

Kim had texted her right back, so she knew she was awake.

Maybe this wasn't the best idea, since Bev couldn't seem to wipe the smile off her face. The evening had been better than anything she could remember since she'd been with Bill before. He just had that way of making her feel beautiful and special and interesting. Fascinating maybe.

Still, even though Iva May was slowly declining, and her death was imminent, this hadn't been a sad house, and no one would be offended over her smile.

Going softly, just in case Kim had fallen asleep since Bev had texted her, she slipped into the kitchen where the hospital bed was set up, slowly closing the door behind her and glancing around the kitchen, thankful for the twinkle lights that Bill had put up.

She was able to find Kim's gaze easily as she sat beside her mother.

Kim's brows had raised, almost as though asking about the smile on Bev's face.

Kim didn't look sad, although she did seem tired. Her shoulders drooped some as she sat holding Iva May's hand.

Bev walked in, taking a chair on the opposite side of Iva May and holding Iva May's other hand.

"Couldn't sleep?" Kim asked softly.

"No," Bev said, keeping her voice down but knowing that Iva May had been sleeping more and more and would not wake easily.

During the day, sometimes they talked in their regular voices, and Iva May never moved.

"How's she been doing?"

"Same. She hasn't eaten since dinnertime, didn't wake up for supper."

"I see." Her heart sank in her chest, and she prayed softly that God would heal Iva May and let them have her for another couple of decades. It was a selfish prayer, since Iva May was ready to go, but Bev wasn't ready to let her.

"She doesn't seem to be in any pain. The hospice nurse said that if she is okay, we don't have to give her morphine, because that seems to make her sleepy. And so I haven't been. She's just...sleeping," Kim said, raising her shoulder.

"I'm so grateful she doesn't seem to be hurting. That would be awful, if she were complaining that she was in pain. So hard if we couldn't do anything for it. If the morphine wouldn't touch it."

"I've been thanking God for that every day that we've been here. I mean, as deaths go, this has been a good one."

Bev nodded, agreeing. "I feel like God's rewarding her for a good life."

"I suppose. Although, I think there are good people who have hard deaths; it's like one last trial."

"Everybody's going to do it." Bev sighed. "Iva May has been a really good example to me. Her submission to God's will, her acceptance, and how she's turned her eyes toward heaven. I don't know if I can do it."

"Me either. She's always been a great example, and you're right. She's leaving us one last thing to remember. How to die well." Kim smiled sadly as she placed a hand on her stomach.

"I'm glad she was able to know about the baby. I can't really think about it, because it makes me sad that she'll never see it. Are you doing okay?" Bev didn't know what grief did to a baby or a pregnant woman. Whether it would cause any lasting problems or not.

"I'm fine. Mom and I have had some long talks. One of the things I've always loved about her is her wisdom. I've been writing some things down she's said about raising children, and I gave her a hard time because I wish she would have written a book." Kim huffed out a breath. "It'd be so nice to have a manual for raising children. You know, do this, and your kids will turn out well."

"Exactly." If only. Raising kids would be so much easier.

"Mom seemed to have a natural knowledge of what to do, but she told me she just read a lot of books written by Christians who did what the Bible says. There are so many Christian books out there that deviate from the Bible when the Bible doesn't go along with what the world thinks."

"That's true."

"Mom gave me the names of some good ones. But I also have some of her observations."

"She always said you were a good kid. It might be different if you have to raise a child who is fussy or strong-willed."

"I hope I don't. Mom said I have Bill's personality."

Bev nodded. Kim certainly didn't have hers. She was the very definition of strong-willed. She always had been. And Bill, he was strong but strongly rooted. He was flexible, relaxed, but unmovable.

"Bill's a good man."

Kim didn't say anything for a while, rubbing her finger over Iva May's wrist and watching it.

Eventually she looked up and said, "As soon as Mom told me about you and Bill, and the babies in the hospital, one of them being me, I knew in my heart she was right. All I need to do is look at you, and I could relate, just felt a connection, that I don't have with any other adult." She raised her brows and looked down. "I know that sounds kind of hocusy-pocusy. I hope I'm not scaring you. I don't usually have premonitions or anything."

"No. I know what you mean. I can't say that I felt anything like that. I guess I was just really wrapped up in myself when it happened. But that just goes to show you that I would have been a terrible mom, because all I thought about was me."

"My mom said you would have been an excellent mom. She felt bad for not stepping forward and at least demanding a paternity test or something. But all those years ago, the technology wasn't as good as it is now, and those things were expensive. Nobody had much money."

"We didn't. And I don't know. I don't know if I would have thought about it, or...what I would have done. Because honestly, I thought about giving my baby up for adoption. If I could have chosen an adoptive mother, Iva May would have been the one."

"Yeah. I've been blessed. But anyway, I've been thinking."

"Yeah?" Bev said, catching a note in Kim's voice that made her heart skip a beat and then start pounding.

"I... I don't really know how people go about these things." She laughed a little. "I've never seen anyone quite in our situation before. But... I'd really like to get to know you and Bill. I know we haven't talked much, not about parentage and the possibility of me being your child, and at forty, it's a little bit tough to think that my whole life has been a lie."

"Not a lie. Just the beginning was not as nailed down as what you thought."

Kim smiled a little. "That's a good way of putting it. I guess I did have a little bit of anger at times. That Mom couldn't have at least told me that there was some question. But she said that she was afraid that I would choose to be with you, because you were rich."

"I wouldn't have allowed it." Bev knew in her heart that that was true. She wouldn't have allowed Kim to choose her over Iva May just because of money.

"Well, teenagers are notorious for not having good judgment."

"I'm the poster child for that," Bev said, raising her hand a little. After all, she had a baby at fifteen. She'd lied to her boyfriend about her age. And then, she hadn't even noticed that the baby who had died might not even have been hers. If she weren't so pathetic, she could almost laugh at how dumb she was.

"I'd like to say I would never have chosen money over Mom and her wisdom, but... I don't know. Sometimes I think I might have. After all, we could never afford vacations, or the fancy clothes that everyone else seemed to wear, or even a nice car."

Bev knew Bill had made sure that Iva May had plenty, but Iva May had been content having just enough, and anything beyond just enough, she'd given away. Bev had admired that for years, and now, she was kind of thinking it was a good idea.

"When you have a lot of money, you have to spend a lot of time managing it. The different funds it's in, different investments, it takes your time. You check your bank account, you look and see whether it's grown. You start to panic when it's not growing as fast as what you think it should, or if it gets below a certain point, even though that certain point would have been an amazing amount to you just a year prior. I'm not sure it's worth it. Honestly. I've been thinking about giving all of my...wealth, I guess you could call it, away."

"Seriously?" Kim said, as though her mother giving money away was normal but to hear Bev talk about it was astounding.

"I think Iva May touched us all. And like I said, having money is stress, although up to a certain point, it does relieve stress. When you don't have to worry about how you're going to pay your bills."

"Yeah," Kim said softly.

"How are you doing in that area, can I ask?"

Kim actually smiled, which surprised Bev. She felt like she was prying. Like she was asking a question that might be too probing and might cause emotional distress, especially as her mom lay dying between them. Kim's smile really threw her.

"I was just saying, trying to say, Mom and I have been talking, and I really wanted to know how to get to know you and Bill better. There's no protocol for this type of thing. I'm the only person I know in this situation, although I'm sure there are other instances. I'm just not personally acquainted with anyone. And I wasn't sure...how, as a forty-year-old, I go about forming a mother-daughter relationship and a father-daughter relationship. It feels like it will be awkward and uncomfortable. But..." Kim lifted her eyes, her face sincere, hopeful. "I really want to."

Bev could count on one hand the number of times she'd cried in her life. And that was no joke. She did not cry over everything, or anything. And she definitely didn't cry over someone else's words.

But Kim's words brought tears to her eyes, and she had to take several deep breaths before she trusted herself enough to say, "Thank you. That probably means more to me than anything you could have said. I want a relationship, but I didn't want to push. Iva May deserves your love, whether she's blood or not. She sacrificed for you, and she's raised a beautiful daughter, a successful adult. I... I feel a little bit like I'm taking from her if I step in as a mom at this point."

"Mom was going to say something to you about that. She didn't want you to feel that way at all. In fact, she was rather adamant that you not feel that way. She wanted you to feel welcome to be as much of a part of my life as you wanted to and as I wanted, which I had told her that I wanted as much of you as I can get. After all, I have two amazing women as my moms. How blessed can a girl get?"

Bev was feeling very blessed herself. After all, Kim could have had a completely different reaction. Especially since the only woman she'd known as her mom was so near death. But instead, Kim had chosen to look at things in the very best light possible. She'd chosen to forgive Bev for not paying more attention to her baby, not noticing that the one that was dead wasn't the one she'd been handed when it was born.

"Iva May raised a beautiful and wise woman," Bev finally said softly.

Kim smiled sadly, her hands still on her stomach. "I'm not feeling very wise. I haven't for a while. I made a huge mistake, because of anger and vindictiveness. I thought I would be getting my ex back, but instead, I just managed to hurt myself more. And create a child that doesn't have a secure home. I feel stupid."

"Don't do that. Please. We all make mistakes. I've made a bunch. I think, more than making mistakes, it's how we react to them after we've made them, the choices we make when we're down, that show our wisdom. Since everyone, especially in the heat of the moment, does stupid things."

"I know. I just feel like I'm old enough to know better. Old enough to have control of myself. Old enough to walk away with dignity, instead of getting down and acting just as bad, if not worse, than my ex."

"Do you know what you're going to do? Are you going to live here?" Bev asked, not knowing the details of what Kim had done but not wanting to pry. She didn't want to know any sordid tales anyway. She loved her and respected her, and figured that everyone had the capacity to make terrible, horrible mistakes.

"Aunt Tricia is really fighting for the house."

"Oh! I just assumed you'd get it. I was planning on moving to Blueberry Beach permanently, and Bill and I..."

She didn't finish her sentence, but the sadness disappeared from Kim's face and she smiled.

"You and Bill are an obvious match. Everyone can see it, except apparently you two. You can't be in the same room together without, not physical sparks, but some kind of electricity flowing between you two. I've always noticed it, even before I knew you were a thing when you were younger."

"Really? I was trying to avoid him."

"Maybe that's why. Maybe you can feel it too."

Bev nodded slowly. There had always been something magnetic about Bill for her. She hadn't realized it was something that other people could see or notice.

"We went out on a date tonight."

"I thought that's why you were smiling when you walked in. That's probably why you can't sleep either," Kim said with a knowing grin.

"Most definitely. He's...he's a good man. A very good man. Far better than what I deserve."

"Don't sell yourself short. I don't disagree that Bill is an amazing man. Mom has been telling me about him—and you—for the last few days every time I sit with her, and she has nothing but glowing things to say about you guys. It makes me proud to be your daughter."

Bev looked at the woman lying silently on the bed. Even in death, with its specter looming, Iva May had been planting seeds of kindness and love. There were surely stories she could have told Kim about the bad things that Bev and Bill had done. Both of them surely had mistakes in their past, things they weren't proud of, things they wished they could do over.

Bev knew she did.

But instead of talking about those things, Iva May had been emphasizing the good. Because she wanted to pave the way for Bev and Bill to both have a parent-child relationship with Kim.

She was astounded again at Iva May's total lack of self, her deep humility. After all, she could have been worried either that Kim might not consider her her mom anymore or want to cling even closer to her as she passed from life to death. She wouldn't have any way of drawing her near after she passed, so she could have been trying to tie the apron strings as tight as she could.

Instead, it looked like she'd been loosening them. Letting Kim go. Giving her a little launch out of Iva May's nest and into a nest that hadn't even been built yet, if Bev and Bill ended up together.

"I think I can speak for Bill when I say that both of us will be absolutely ecstatic to have you consider us your parents. And we will always be absolutely grateful to Iva May for all the work that she's done. I don't want to take a single bit of credit from her, because she deserves it all."

"She sure does."

Bev came back to the subject she'd let go at first but wanted to make clear. "I don't think you even need to fight your Aunt Tricia for the house. The will should be very clear, since you're her daughter."

"That's what Mom said. But I don't want to fight. And Mom has a small cottage up at Strawberry Sands. I feel pulled to there. I ... I love Blueberry Beach. I don't want to leave, but I just can't see myself fighting over money, material things. Life is too short for me to stand here with my hands on my hips demanding what I deserve and fighting with Aunt Tricia."

"Your mom definitely deserves the credit for that, because I wouldn't have raised you to be like that. But that's the exact way you should be. If you are meant to have a house here at Blueberry Beach, God will work it out. And you won't need to fight your family for it."

Bev was impressed despite herself at the maturity of Kim and her total acceptance of giving away the house in Blueberry Beach, which was actually worth something, and not fighting for what was rightfully hers, and taking the small and—if Bev remembered correctly—rundown cottage in the less affluent, although equally beautiful, Strawberry Sands.

"I can't help but think that maybe Strawberry Sands needs something I can contribute." Kim shrugged her shoulders. "I have no idea what that might be. But it's just as pretty as Blueberry Beach and just fifteen minutes north. So just a little farther from Chicago. Why isn't it as prosperous? Maybe God has something for me to do up there? Maybe not even pertaining to business, but maybe there are people out there that need me. I've determined that I won't fight Aunt Tricia, and if she demands the house as her right, I'm gonna trust that God wants me in Strawberry Sands for a reason."

"Wow. I admire that. That ability to see that maybe what seems so unfair and not right could actually be the Lord working out something better for you."

"Well, Mom deserves a lot of the credit, because we've been talking about it. And although she insisted that this house should be mine, she also said that maybe there was a possibility that God wanted me somewhere else, and that's what got me thinking. Which led to that decision."

"I hadn't realized your Aunt Tricia was still around. I've not seen her since she was here when I was here."

Kim nodded. "She comes almost every day. If Mom's awake, she treats Aunt Tricia so well, but if Mom's sleeping, you can just see her hands clench and her teeth will grind together. You can tell that Aunt Tricia upsets her."

"Probably because she's trying to take from you."

"Yeah. That's what I figured. If there was one thing that gets Mom's dander up, it was people being unkind to me."

"I remember. People could say the worst things about your mom, treat her so badly, when she was waitressing at the diner or any of the other things she did, and over the years, I remember a couple, several, times where rumors flew around, and people weren't nice. Iva May always took it with a smile. But when someone said something about you..." Bev laughed. "She was like a grizzly bear. One of the doctors from the hospital in Chicago owned a vacation house near here and was well known in our community. He wasn't necessarily well-liked, but his family was good. Anyway, do you remember he stopped you in the street?"

"I do. And he started telling me how terrible my mom was because she didn't wait on his table fast enough, and then she added his bill up wrong, and he called her a cheat and a liar and a lazy witch, and he started telling me that she wasn't really a Christian, and...I started to cry."

"I remember. Your mom saw him accosting you through the window, and I'm pretty sure if Bill hadn't seen what was happening too and grabbed a hold of your mom, I think she would have ripped that doctor's throat out."

"I think she would have too. And he hadn't touched me. All he'd done was be unkind to me and make me cry." Kim smiled a little at the memory. "I've never seen my mom that angry. I didn't even know she got angry. It shocked me. And...can I admit I was a little disappointed?"

"Disappointed?" Bev asked, surprised.

"Yeah. After all, Mom was pretty much perfect. The idea that she could get that angry, and be that... I don't know, mean, maybe. Not that she said anything unkind. She just acted like she wanted to kill him. Her face... She looked so angry. Anyway, I understand, after having my own child, how a mother could do that, but at the time, I wondered, because up until that point, she always lived everything she preached. Everything. She'd been perfect. And yet there she was, almost committing murder right beside the diner."

"A mother's bond with her child is really strong," Bev said, knowing it was true. "And Iva May loved you with her whole heart and soul."

"I know. And I can't deny that it made me feel good that someone was going to stick up for me. It made me confident. Even though that incident opened my eyes in some ways, I felt like no matter what I did, my mom was in my corner. I knew she'd go to bat for me, although I also knew that if I was wrong, she'd let me face the consequences and not try to manipulate things so that I got out of punishment that I deserved."

"The very best kind of parenting," Bev said.

"Yeah. I wasn't the best mom, with Alyssa, but I tried to be like my mom was and listen to her advice. Now, I guess God's giving me another chance."

They lapsed into silence, and Bev sat there for another hour before Kim slowly leaned back on her chair, and her soft breathing told her she was asleep too.

Bev slipped out, thinking about giving to others, giving up what was rightfully hers, but also being the kind of person who had wisdom that could help others.

Chapter 19

"She had such a good day yesterday," Bev explained softly to the hospice nurse as she set her electronic pad down and stood beside Iva May's hospital bed. "I know we must have tired her out, and that's why she's not awake yet. But..." Bev's eyes shone as she looked over at Bill.

Bill tried to return her excited look, but he had a premonition. He held his breath while Bev continued.

"It's funny that she felt so good. She actually got out of bed for the first time in several weeks. And it coincided with the January thaw, so the temperatures were almost up to sixty. We wrapped her in a blanket and put her in her wheelchair and took her out on the front porch."

"It was so much fun," Kim added, smiling and speaking softly as well. "We had the whole town of Blueberry Beach there. They actually closed the diner down to the public, and Bill cooked hot dogs and hamburgers to feed everyone. It was like a big party, and Mom was laughing and talking to people and just having a great time."

The hospice nurse's face held a smile, but her look said the same thing that Bill's heart said.

"I'm really hopeful that this is an answer to prayer and that she's going to wake up healed. Or at least be on her way to healing. That God will take the cancer away, and she'll have another ten or twenty or thirty years with us." Bev spoke with so much hope in her voice that Bill actually felt his eyes prick. He busied himself by turning to the sink and rinsing his coffee cup out because he didn't want her to see his face.

"Don't you agree?" Bev finally asked the nurse, who hadn't said anything.

"We'll see how today goes. I don't want to be the bearer of bad tidings, but I believe we told you at the initial consultation that as death approaches, sometimes they have one last hurrah, if you will. Just a day of excessive energy and just like you described. And then..."

"The end?" Kim whispered softly.

The hospice nurse nodded.

Both Bev and Kim seemed to take the news in stride as Bill turned from the sink, watching them carefully.

Hospice had been amazing, answering all their questions and never giving more than they could handle. The nurse didn't do so now either but waited to see if they would ask questions.

"How will we know?" Bev asked slowly. Of the two of them, Bev was always the one who wanted more information, while Kim was more content to walk in darkness.

Made sense since that matched Bev's more aggressive personality. She wanted to know all the facts and information so she could make informed decisions, while Kim would rather protect herself and be happy, not facing any catastrophes until they happened.

Over the past few weeks since Christmas, Bill had noticed more and more physical similarities and even similar mannerisms between Bev and Kim, but it was obvious that Kim had gotten his more laid-back personality.

The hospice nurse looked at Iva May, pulled on her earring, and then she said, "Sometimes their skin, especially down on their feet, becomes mottled as death approaches."

Kim walked over to her mom and carefully pulled the blanket back, exposing her feet.

"Yes. Like that," the nurse said gently as they looked at the mottling, dark and obvious, on both of Iva May's legs and feet.

Kim flipped the blanket back in place.

"I heard this when I came in," the hospice nurse said softly. "If you listen, you can hear a rattle when she breathes out. We call it the death rattle. Not to be morbid," she said carefully, watching Bev and Kim as she spoke, almost as though she would stop speaking if she thought she was saying too much.

Bill wanted her to keep talking. He would rather know than not, but it was probably because he wanted to have the information and face it, and not allow it to manipulate him.

Both Kim and Bev nodded as they listened to Iva May breathe, and Bill couldn't believe he hadn't noticed it before.

"Has she gotten up yet this morning at all?" the nurse asked.

"No. We tucked her in about three o'clock yesterday afternoon, because she was tired from all of the visits, and she hasn't moved since."

"Yes. I would say, if you want to call the family in so they're here...at the end... This would be a good time." The nurse put a hand on Kim's shoulder as she spoke, and Kim lifted wide, frightened eyes to Bill, like the news, while it hadn't been unexpected—they'd been looking for it for more than a month—still surprised her.

Bill moved over, putting an arm around Kim's shoulder as the hospice nurse dropped her hand.

"I could be wrong. I have been before. Plenty of people defy our expectations."

"Has anyone ever been this close and come back?" Bill asked, speaking for the first time.

He didn't have to give details, and the nurse knew exactly what he was saying.

"I've heard stories. But I've never seen it myself."

Bill nodded.

While they were standing there, Iva May's cat, Cobbler, surprised everyone by jumping up on Iva May's bed, ignoring everyone standing around her, and walking to Iva May's side, where she sniffed for a moment, then turned in a circle and lay down.

"I've seen that before too," the hospice nurse said. "Animals seem to know when it's time. Has she slept there before?" She turned to face the three adults surrounding her.

They all shook their heads. Normally, Cobbler was very shy and didn't come out if there was company in the house.

As much as Bill had been at Iva May's over the years, he'd barely ever seen Cobbler and usually not unless Iva May went looking for her and brought her out.

One time, Iva May had gone on vacation for a week, and Bill had come and cleaned the litter box and fed her and hadn't seen her the entire time. If it weren't for the waste in the litter box, he would have worried that she'd gotten out somehow.

The nurse did a little more checking, a few more murmurs, confirming her diagnosis, "Her pulse is very slow" and "I didn't take her temperature, but her skin feels cool." She said they were all signs that point to death.

It was almost a relief when she left, although she had been beautifully kind and sweet. Bill figured Kim and Bev felt the same way he did. They just wanted to be alone with Iva May.

"Do you really think this could be the end?" Kim asked from one side where she held Iva May's hand.

"It seems like it," Bev said, her eyes downcast, looking at Iva May's face as though willing her to wake up and say something.

"I don't even remember what her last words were," Kim said sadly. "I was so happy yesterday, tucking her in bed and assuming she'd wake up feeling exactly the way she had yesterday, today."

"Maybe she will." But Bev's voice lacked conviction. They'd been talking around her all morning, and the hospice nurse had come and gone, and she hadn't even woken up.

"Would you like to take a walk?" Bill asked, looking at Bev. Thinking that maybe Kim would need a few minutes alone with her mom.

"Kim?" she asked, leaning her head down to catch Kim's eye. "Will you be okay here alone?"

"I'd actually like that. I... I might never get to talk to my mom again, and I don't know whether she can hear me or not, but I suppose I have a few things to say to her."

"That's fine. We'll be gone..." She looked up at Bill. "How long?"

"An hour? Two?" Bill said, glancing at Kim to try to judge how she seemed to take the suggestion.

"Whatever. Just a few minutes is fine... However long you're gone, it doesn't matter. I'll text you if there are any changes."

"Sounds good. We'll aim for an hour, but we'll watch for a text."

Kim nodded, and Bev stood from her chair, walking over and grabbing a jacket.

The January thaw had stretched to that morning, with temperatures in the mid-fifties.

Some snow had melted, and the ground squished under their feet as they left the house and walked along the back path, down to the beach.

They walked in silence for a while. Bill supposed Bev didn't really feel like romance any more than he did, but he took her hand anyway and she allowed it.

The last few weeks since their date had been busy, with Bev making a trip to Detroit and a convention at the Blueberry Beach Hotel causing Bill to open his shop and also help as a short-order cook at the diner, dealing with the unexpected influx of people.

Bill had taken some overnight watches for Iva May at that point, and Kim hadn't left Iva May's side during the day.

Those weeks had felt long at the time, but looking back, they seemed to have flown by, each day having Iva May getting more tired, sleeping longer, less aware of her surroundings.

That was why yesterday had been so exciting for them with Iva May having energy and, while not quite her normal self, seeming so much better than the previous weeks had been.

"You knew all along yesterday was just an illusion," Bev finally said, and her voice sounded flat and discouraged.

"I remember the first time hospice was here, at the initial consultation, they mentioned there would be a bump at the end. Or that there often was a bump at the end. And I remember up in the UP, growing up on the farm, seeing that in the animals we had. You'd be working on an animal, and they just kept getting sicker and sicker, and then one day, they get up and you think that everything you'd been doing was finally going to work, and then later that day, they'd be dead."

"Seems so final."

"It's not."

"I know. It just...just makes you see how quickly time passes."

Bill had been thinking the exact same thing. As he'd gotten older, he got more patient, more willing to wait, less demanding that things had to happen now. He drove slower, ate slower, talked slower.

But the one thing he hadn't wanted to do slower was his relationship with Bev. He wanted it settled, and now.

"You know how pretty horses would be on the beach?" Bev said, her words sounding dreamy and taking Bill a little by surprise, since they'd been talking about Iva May and aging and that's where his mind was.

But she seemed to have totally changed the subject.

He could get on board with that.

"You know the cottage Iva May owns up on Strawberry Sands is perfect for horses, if I remember correctly. I was there a few years ago doing some repairs for her, and there's a paddock and a small shelter like they boarded horses there before."

He supposed he was just making conversation, since that's where he thought of when she'd mentioned horses.

"Kim told me that she was planning on moving there."

"She's not taking the house?"

"No. She and I had a discussion about it a few weeks ago, and I asked her about it just a couple of nights ago, again. She told me it was okay to talk to you about it, because she was pretty sure that's what she was going to do."

"What is she going to do with Iva May's house here at Blueberry Beach?" Bill couldn't keep the incredulity out of his voice. He'd never thought of Kim living anywhere else.

"Her Aunt Tricia, Iva May's sister-in-law, is demanding it be hers. And technically, according to Kim, it was in her father's family."

"Even if Iva May didn't have a will, everything should go to Kim."

"Kim knows that. She's already been in touch with a lawyer because she said she didn't want to fight."

"Not while Iva May is alive and can hear."

"Not then, and not after. Because she knows that's what Iva May wants... She also knows that's what's right. Sometimes, it's better to do right than be right. At least, that's what Kim basically told me. And if Aunt Tricia wants the house, she's going to give it to her."

"Wow. I think of Christianity as giving people cups of cold water on a hot summer day or buying someone a Pepsi. Not giving them a *house*. Surely that's going a little bit above and beyond what Jesus wants us to do."

"Do you really think so?" Bev stopped walking and turned toward him.

The breeze off the lake was chilly but not frigid the way it had been the past two months, and it felt refreshing to Bill, who said, "Maybe I should just shave my head."

Chapter 20

"That's a subject change." Bev blinked.

"I felt the hair on my head stirring, and I think when you can feel each individual strand moving, it's probably time to just kiss the whole thing goodbye. All ten strands that are left up there." Bill tilted his head at her, enjoying that they had become closer since Iva May's diagnosis. "Do you mind being with me if I'm bald?"

"I think we've already had this discussion. Back on our date. You told me I was beautiful. And I think I told you you needed glasses."

Bill shook his head. "No. I'm already wearing them anyway, but I know you didn't say that to me."

"I guess I just thought you needed your prescription changed."

"You're not answering the question. Maybe I should go sacrifice a sheep or something and glue a patch of sheepskin on my head."

She laughed. "No. You're perfect the way you are."

"I guess the house isn't too much to give. You're right." He went back to their former subject, having just needed to have a little bit of time to run it over in his mind.

She was right. Kim was right. Iva May was right.

"If you think about it, you've given away a house."

"I've never given away a house."

"When you sold the family property in the UP and moved down here. You put that money in a separate fund, and that's what you've used any time you've done something good for someone else. Have you used all the money?" she asked, and he understood it wasn't because she wanted to know if he still had money. She was asking if he had given away the whole house.

"Oh. I see what you mean. They got about ten million for the property, and I still have three million in the bank. But..." He wasn't going to say this to her, but since she brought it up. "I've been in the process of talking to my accountant and figuring out the best way to gift that to you."

"What?"

They had started walking again, but Bev stopped short and spun to him.

"You're gifting it to me? Why?"

"Wow. She sounds grateful."

"It's not that I'm not grateful, it's that that's crazy."

"Well, not really."

"I'm sorry. You thought Kim giving away the house was crazy. Iva May's house is not worth three million dollars."

"I wouldn't be so sure. Since the hospital went in and the businesses around it have been growing, property values around Blueberry Beach have really been increasing. It might be worth that much."

Bev made a sound that could be agreement.

"I mentioned that I had talked to Pastor Kane a while back?"

"Yes. Around Christmas, I think."

"He gave me some advice on things I could do for you. Things that I messed up on or don't think about. It's not that I don't care, it's just that I want you to know how important you are to me."

"You've been doing little things," she said, her cheeks reddening, as she turned her head and started walking again.

He started with her, never letting go of her hand.

"You put blankets on me when I fell asleep beside Iva May, carried me to the couch. Made coffee for me in the morning, and you know how I like my coffee made, I don't even have to tell you or ask."

"Yeah. I always considered myself a kind person, but sometimes I wasn't always thoughtful."

"No. You're perfect."

"But I can keep trying to get better. I want the people who are in my life to know that they're important to me. Sometimes the things I do that I think show you you're important don't say to you what I think they do."

He didn't give her a chance to say anything, because he didn't want her to have to look hard to see the things that he did. He wanted them to be meaningful to her. Otherwise, it was more her appreciating him than him showing appreciation.

"I know in my last marriage, my wife said I put my work ahead of her. But she also said I put other people ahead of her. I never understood that. I mean, I had to keep my business going, that's how I pay for things. But the thing was, she saw all the money I had in the bank, and even though she knew it was earmarked for charities, and I never spent a dime on myself, she didn't think we should have to live on a shop-keeper's salary when I was actually a millionaire."

This time, he did pause. It felt odd to call himself a millionaire, but he'd been one all of his life. Although, the millions were slowly dwindling.

"I wanted to avoid that with you. So I'm just giving you the money."

Bev stopped again, only this time, she sort of slowed to a halt. And she didn't turn to face him but had her eyes downcast on the sand, her hair blowing in a gust of wind. She tugged her hand away and wrapped her arms around herself, almost as though his comment had made her uncomfortable or made her notice the cold.

"So you're trying to buy me?" she finally said.

"No!"

That wasn't what he was doing at all. He couldn't believe she thought that.

"I don't want you to think other people are more important than you are. When I say you're the most important, I want you to see with my actions that I mean it. Every word."

"Maybe you should have waited until we were married? We might not end up together."

"I'm at the point in my life where I know what I want. I want you. Or I don't want anyone. If you decide that there isn't going to be an 'us,' then I'm going to decide to be happy as a single shopkeeper in Blueberry Beach."

"You won't have the money you used to have, so when you see a need, you won't be able to meet it."

"That'll be a change. But it wasn't always about the money. Sometimes people just need a body. They need someone to fill in as a short-order cook. They need someone to fix their cottage in a different town. They need someone to sit on the sidewalk in the evening and talk about life and dispense wisdom. They need someone to love their children. Someone to talk about the way things used to be and how we can do things better." He shrugged. "I can still do all of those things. And I wouldn't have done this if I didn't want you to have the money."

"I guess you're old enough to know what you want," Bev agreed.

They weren't walking, they weren't looking at each other, they were just standing, two separate people whose lives had intersected over the years, and now they were looking at their golden years, the end of their working years, the beginning of retirement, this time when the rest of the world told them that they should relax, take it easy, do things for themselves. Bill didn't buy that. Never had.

Just because a person was retired from their job didn't mean they retired from the Christian life. Didn't mean they retired from serving others. Being a blessing.

He thought of Iva May and how she'd lived her life to the very end working for others. "Do you suppose Iva May has money put back?"

"It wouldn't surprise me at all. She lived very simply. And from what I can gather, her husband wasn't very nice, but he had a lot."

"You wouldn't know to look at her."

"No. You wouldn't. She's...humble."

"And generous. I was always having her give away my money, but now I wonder if she didn't add some of her own every time."

"I know she did several times, just because I was involved." Bev's mouth closed as Bill studied her.

"You mean, you handled some of Iva May's donations?"

Bev gave a side glance, then she nodded. "No one knows. And I'm not supposed to tell. Iva May didn't want people knowing what she'd done. She said, 'I can either have the accolades here, or I can store up treasure in heaven where I can never lose it. That's what I want.'"

"Maybe that's another reason she's looking forward to going to heaven. 'For where your treasure is, there will your heart be also.'"

"Exactly." Bev reached out to squeeze his hand, then tugged on it until they were facing each other, their shoulders to the lake and the stiff breeze as she took a step closer, putting a hand on his waist. "Were you serious when you said that you knew what you wanted and what you wanted was me?"

"Yes. You're the one I want. You've always been the one I wanted. Some things never change."

"Our lives aren't getting any longer. Every second that expires is one we'll never get back."

"It's been that way all our lives."

"Then color me slow, because it feels like now, while I agree with you, I'm more patient than I used to be, a little better at keeping my mouth shut than when I was younger, more apt to be forgiving of others and less judgmental. But I feel like every day we're not together is a day I can't get back and a day that's wasted."

Bill's throat closed, and his heart seemed to be beating out of his chest. He wanted to answer her. Wanted to say he felt the same way, but there just seemed to be a logjam in his mouth which was dry and felt like it was stuffed with cotton balls, and he couldn't get anything out.

"I don't want you to think it's because of the money. That's just a tiny bit of what I have, although, I want to be like Iva May. I don't want to build a big mansion on the hill somewhere and live in the lap of luxury for the rest of my life." She paused. "Although I do want to have indoor toilets, electricity, and all that."

He loved that she was joking a little since this whole conversation felt so serious to him. His throat eased.

"We're compatible in that area," he said. Maybe his voice was just a little bit gruff, but at least he was talking.

"So I don't know. I don't know what I want to do with my money, but I know what I want to do with my life. I want to spend what's left of it, and it could be decades or more, with you."

"I think she just asked me to marry her."

She laughed. "Well, you asked me all those years ago. And I know I said that this time I was going to wait on you, just follow your lead, but I figured in that area, it was my turn to take the lead, since I pushed for everything else, but when you talked about marriage, I froze." Her lip pulled back. "I was afraid. I'm still afraid."

"I'm not. That's an easy yes for me. I'm not afraid."

"Not afraid of you. Or of marriage necessarily, or even the whole making a vow I'm planning to keep until I die. That's easy. It's the...the vulnerability. The..."

"Nakedness. You're scared of the nakedness."

He grinned and she smiled, but not quite as big.

"Yeah. Basically."

Bill figured there were probably other things that happened as a woman aged that maybe she was concerned about as well, but she was wasting her time worrying about anything.

"I suppose if I were a gentleman, I would tell you we don't really need to have nakedness in our marriage, but...I guess I'm not as much of a gentleman as I thought I was."

Her eyes had brightened when he had mentioned about not needing nakedness, then she laughed when he finished his sentence. "I have to say, you had me excited there for a minute."

"I would have been disappointed. Do not make me do that, please."

"Of course not. That thought never even crossed my mind."

"Should we set a date?"

"Yeah."

"Do you want a big wedding?" he asked, and he tried to make his voice sound like he didn't care. And truly, if that's what she wanted, he'd try to go along.

"No. I don't want anything pretentious. I don't want anything we have to plan and wait for. We've made a decision to get married, and I don't want to mess around. Let's get it done."

"It's not like a job you have to get out of your way."

"I'm sorry. I didn't mean it like that. I meant it like we made a decision, we don't want to sit around and rethink it. I want to make it and then move forward with it. That's how I feel about this."

"Doesn't feel very romantic to me," he teased. "I've been working on being more romantic, and this isn't fitting into the picture I've created of what romance is."

"I suppose you're not the only one who needs to improve yourself. Because I can use work. Are you going to give me lessons in romance?"

He laughed at the idea of him being able to teach anyone how to be romantic. "I think probably in all honesty, I would really like to know what you think about romance and how I can be better at it. I know that's one area I'm lacking."

"I think you've made steps on your own. I'm not unhappy."

"Does that mean we can't talk about it?"

"Not at all. That just means I don't feel like you need to change yourself in order for me to love you."

Bill stopped mid-breath. They'd talked about it before he even kissed her, but then they got busy, and while he felt confident taking her hand, covering her with a blanket, and even carrying her to the couch, they hadn't really talked any more, and that date almost seemed like a dream to him.

Now they were getting married.

"What are you laughing at?" she asked, curiously but also with concern in her eyes. After all, the conversation had been serious.

"I'm just thinking that after our date, I was pretty excited about our relationship, and then... We just got busy, and it almost feels like it wasn't real. And now we're getting married. Talk about not feeling real."

"Oh." Her voice was a little subdued.

He ran over in his head what he might have done, and he realized he'd laughed at a really bad time and missed an opportunity to be romantic. He wasn't sure if he could get it back.

"I love you. I love talking to you. I love laughing with you. I love listening to you. I love the way the things you say bring other things to mind, and I feel like I could talk to you forever. I don't feel like I need to change myself for you to love me. But I want to change myself to be better, because a woman as wonderful as you deserves the very best man on the planet, and I'm far, far from that. But I want you to have what you deserve, and I'll never stop working to be better, never stop appreciating the fact that you took me even when I wasn't good enough for you."

Bev's eyes had started to fill, which surprised him, and he bit the inside of his cheek, wondering if he had gone too far. He thought she needed all the pretty words, but maybe those weren't good tears, and he didn't know what he'd done wrong.

"Please don't cry," he finally said, when she seemed to be fighting to speak.

"I can't help it. That was beautiful. It's something I've always wanted to hear, but it's not true. Not true at all."

"It is true. And we laugh at how I'm not romantic."

"That doesn't make up who you are. It's your character, it's your determination to do right. It's your patience and your consideration and kindness and even just what you were saying, your willingness to change to be better, because you don't think you're good enough for me. That's beautiful. But it's not true. And I love your humility, just for the record."

"Can I be proud of my humility?" he asked, just because he wanted to say something that wasn't hard and deep and that would keep her from crying, because he couldn't take it.

"I think you have plenty of room to be proud of your humility, because you're pretty much the most humble man I've ever met."

"I know that's not true, but I guess I appreciate your admiration. It makes me feel it right here." He hit his chest. "To think that you admire things about me. I... I guess I don't really care what the rest of the world thinks, but I'd be lying if I said I didn't care what you think. And I know I'm not all those things you said, but it makes me feel good to think that you think that about me. It also makes me want to work to be those things, because you believe in me."

"I believe in you, because you're worth believing in," she said, her eyes sparkling as she looked up at him.

They already stood close, close enough for him to smell the sweet sassiness that made up her scent mixed with the fresh breeze from the wide waters of Lake Michigan. It was his favorite scent in the entire world.

As his head lowered, he said, "What day did we decide we're getting married?"

"Is it terrible to get married on the day Iva May passes away?"

"I think she sees her passing as a celebration. That's a little bit hard for me to get into, but I honestly think she'd love it. After all, I'm pretty sure that's exactly what she wanted when she called you and me to her house to meet after the Christmas Eve service."

"I bet she didn't think it was going to happen this fast," Bev whispered, her lips so close to his they brushed a little as she spoke.

"Either one, us or her," Bill agreed.

Bev shook her head, her nose brushing his. "I think she knew. I think she believed in us."

Bill smiled, because he thought that was right, but he didn't tell her. He just kissed her instead. A sweet kiss, filled with promises of fresh lake breezes and extended hope for the rest of their lives together.

Epilogue

Kim stood in her mother's living room, at the head of the casket, greeting the people of Blueberry Beach as they filed around. Some folks sat in the chairs that were set out, some sat on the couch. All friends. All people who were familiar to her, whom she loved.

Well, it might be pushing it a little to say she loved her Aunt Tricia. She was *trying* to love her. She sat on the couch next to Gage and his wife, shopkeepers just down the street from the diner, and engaged them in conversation, bragging about things she'd done in her life and the places she'd been, while Gage and his wife nodded politely. Kim got the feeling they would like to be anywhere else.

Other than Tricia's voice, the other sounds were muted murmurings. Respectful, but Kim had made a point to smile and to let people know that her mother considered her death a celebration. A happy time. A time where she was going home and wasn't a stranger in a strange land anymore.

Kim admired her mother's attitude so much and hoped that she could grow to be more like her in the coming years. For the sake of her children. One unborn. She put her hand on her stomach and lifted her eyes just in time to see her other daughter walking in the door with her father.

Her ex-husband had one arm around his daughter, one arm around his new wife, like he was actually a good husband and family man.

The thought made the nausea that was never far from Kim's stomach boil and roll.

She would not throw up at her mother's viewing. Would not.

The words stuck in her head as her averted eyes slid back to the doorway, because someone else followed her husband.

Her heart caught in her throat, and the hand that had been on her stomach rose to her chest, as though to squelch the pain that had suddenly squeezed tight in that area.

Her husband's best friend, Davis. And the father of her baby.

Bev stood at her right side, and Kim leaned over to her. "I need to leave. I need some air."

"Do you want me to come with you?" Bev said, motherly concern for her child in her tone.

Kim smiled at the way the words wrapped around her like a hug. Someday, someday soon, she was going to have to start calling Bev and Bill mom and dad, because they certainly had stepped into those roles as naturally as breathing.

Kim needed to tell them how much she appreciated all they'd done for her, the way they'd been there for her, the way they'd supported her decision to give Aunt Tricia the house, and the way they'd totally been behind her when she said she was moving to Strawberry Sands, along with their offers to help fix up the house and the stable and to help her look into possibly boarding horses and renting them out for people to ride along the beach.

It had been an exciting business opportunity, especially as Blueberry Beach became more and more commercialized, and Strawberry Sands seemed to be the place that people were going for a more natural experience along the lake.

Bill and Bev had rallied the town together in a short amount of time, and despite her mother's death, so many people had told her that they would advertise her business in their places of employment. The ladies who owned the Blueberry Beach Hotel had said they would put it on their brochure and literature in every room.

Kim had been overwhelmed, and of course the town would have taken care of her without Bev and Bill spearheading it, but the fact remained that their main concern had been entirely for her.

She swallowed her nausea and whispered to Bev, "No. I was hoping you would stay here and continue to greet people for me."

Bill had heard them whispering and turned his head, his brows raised.

Bev whispered in his ear, and he nodded.

"Of course," Bev's voice came to her. "We'll stay, but text me if you need me, okay?"

"I will. I... I just need some fresh air. I'm really fine."

She really wanted to stay, wanted to see her daughter and talk to her. Hadn't seen her for months. Alyssa hadn't even been up to see her grandmother, despite Kim's texts and calls. Her ex had successfully poisoned her mind and completely made Kim the bad guy, even though he had been the one who cheated.

She'd been the one who got caught.

Slipping away from the casket and walking down behind a group of people standing in a circle chatting, she slipped down the side, into the hall, and walked outside.

Someday, someday she'd be strong enough to face her ex. To face the woman who cheated with a man she knew to be married. Even to face the man she'd had the one-night stand with. It had been well after her divorce was final, and while fornication was never right, she hadn't been married at the time.

So technically, in the world's eyes at least, she hadn't done anything wrong. Nothing to end her marriage, which had been over and finalized.

Still, she felt guilty, because it was a sin in God's eyes.

And now, she had a precious life to take care of. One she loved deeply and fiercely already.

She didn't want the reminders in front of her.

Although... Davis was a good man, and what he'd done with her that night wasn't something he normally did.

Regardless, she lifted her face to the breeze, facing the lake, able to see just a sliver of it in the distance, and vowed to herself that her first forty years had been lived for herself, but she was going to do better with her next forty years.

They were going to start at a beach cottage in Strawberry Sands, where she'd raise her child, rent out horses on the beach, and do her best to follow the example that her mother had laid down. She couldn't wait to get started.

THANKS SO MUCH FOR reading! If you'd like to preorder Kim's book, **There I Find Peace**, you can get it HERE[1].

If you'd like to interact with me, join my Facebook group[2].

I'd love for you to sign up for my newsletter[3] to read about my daily life on the farm, be the first to know about my new releases, get deals on my books and occasionally get other sweet romance deals as well.

ENJOY THIS PREVIEW of *Cowboy Walking Away*, just for you!

1. https://www.amazon.com/gp/product/B0B753PG95/

2.   https://www.facebook.com/groups/jessiegussman/

3.   https://dl.bookfunnel.com/svgbc8n23d

Cowboy Walking Away
Chapter 1

Good Communication and willingness to forgive. – Mary S., North Carolina

ROSE BALDWIN PUSHED a hair back on her face and wished she were anywhere else.

Anywhere.

Even a snake pit would be better than this.

Laughter cut into her thoughts, and she grabbed the pan of mashed potatoes, taking it to the second table on the right in the church basement in Sweet Water, North Dakota.

The second table on the right was a table that she'd been avoiding as much as she could, all evening.

Since there were only two servers, herself and her sister, for the annual Sweet Water Sweethearts Valentine's Day banquet, she hadn't been able to get out of serving that table even though she truly wanted to.

There were nine other people at the table other than her ex.

One of those people was the woman Harry had left her for, Leah.

Rose set the mashed potatoes down with a smile, at the opposite end of the table from where Harry and Leah were sitting, and grabbed the empty pan.

"I need a refill on my drink," Leah called out before Rose could get away.

Rose's smile felt like her teeth would break, but she nodded and said, "I'll be right back."

"Oh, honey! Take my glass," she called out.

Since Patty's Diner was only catering the event, not hosting it in their restaurant, they weren't bringing new glasses but refilling the old ones.

Rose knew this. She just had a memory lapse, since she worked at Patty's Diner and was used to bringing new glasses with each drink.

"Thank you," she said as she took the glass from Leah, who probably wasn't looking at her in a smug, arrogant kind of way, even though it seemed like she was.

Rose definitely didn't look over at Harry.

Which was quite a feat, since he was sitting so close to Leah, his arm wrapped around her, and Leah was practically pasted to his side.

A person would think after three years of Harry being gone, it wouldn't bother her at all.

The empty potato container in one hand, Leah's glass in the other, Rose strode to the kitchen area where Patty herself was doing dishes in the sink and where the bottles of soda and gallons of water were sitting on the countertop.

"I hope we don't run out of mashed potatoes," Patty said with her back toward Rose. "I don't think we have time to make any more."

"There's a big box of instant mashed potatoes in the cupboard. We could probably use that if we absolutely had to, as long as we replace it," said Lavender, Rose's sister who had volunteered to serve with her, as she brought an empty pan of meatloaf back.

"I hate to do that, because I like to make real mashed potatoes, but you're right. Keep an eye on it and let me know when that pan on the stove is empty."

Lavender glanced at her sister, and Rose said, "We will."

Lavender didn't work at the diner, but when they had needed help to serve the banquet, she'd volunteered, since anyone who had a significant other was at the banquet and help was limited.

Rose took a minute to shove back the hair that had fallen out from underneath the headband she wore along with her ponytail.

Lavender came over, putting her arm around Rose's waist and leaning close to her ear. "The guy's a jerk, and so is she. Don't let them get to you."

"Thanks. He's really not. It's just...this wasn't the way these things were supposed to go." She gave her sister a sidelong glance before she picked up Leah's glass and poured diet soda into it.

"Whether he gets it now, or whether God deals with him in some other way. It's coming. You know that."

"I know. Thanks for reminding me," Rose said as she picked up the glass and walked back out.

Harry had been married to Rose for five years. In that time, Rose had begged to have children, and Harry had put her off, saying he wanted to be more established financially and that they had plenty of time to have kids later.

That was after telling Rose before they were married that he wanted to start a family right away.

It was also before he walked out on Rose and walked into Leah's marriage.

Rose wasn't entirely sure the particulars, since she'd never specifically talked to Harry or Leah about it, but according to Leah's husband Chuck, Leah and Harry were texting long before Leah left. Rose couldn't say for sure Harry had been texting Leah before he walked out on her.

Because she had trusted him, completely, blindly, and, as it turned out, stupidly.

So now, three years later, he acted like he was madly in love with the woman he'd left her for, and they had a happy family of four children, since Leah had three, and they'd immediately had a child of their own as soon as they left their spouses.

While Rose was alone.

She set the glass down in front of Leah and murmured "you're welcome," even though she didn't hear "thank you," and moved to another table where she took an empty plate and a container that needed to be filled up with more bean casserole.

She supposed she didn't have to be alone. She'd been asked out more than once, but...it was just hard to trust anyone after what she'd been through. She really didn't want to, except... Her eyes went to Harry and Leah again. Except they looked so happy together, and that burned her.

That her ex had lied. That he'd cheated, that he'd kept her from having children.

He'd done all of those things, and now he was the one with the big happy family, and she was the one who was alone, even though she was the one who had done right.

God? It's not fair!

She didn't need the Good Lord to remind her that life wasn't fair.

She also didn't need Lavender to remind her that eventually Harry would have to face the Lord where his works would be judged.

She appreciated those reminders though, because sometimes, like now, it was hard not to be bitter.

"Rose!" Charlene called out from beside her sweetheart, Charlie. They were also sitting at the second table on the right.

Rose walked over to the table, reluctantly, unable to turn down a direct request and also unwilling to ignore Charlene, who had been extremely supportive of her and probably knew just as much as her mother did about what had gone on.

Charlene headed up the Sweet Water quilting club and had been instrumental in getting the club to take Rose under their wings for those first few months when she'd been devastated beyond words at Harry's betrayal.

"You look like you're having a great time, Miss Charlene," Rose said, standing so her shoulder was toward Harry and Leah, directly across from Miss Charlene.

"The food is excellent, as always. Miss Patty is a magician in the kitchen," Charlene said, pausing for a moment to wait for Leah's laugh to fade away.

It was probably just Rose's imagination that she had a laugh that could grate on anyone's nerves.

Really, Leah was probably an extremely nice lady. Rose's opinion was biased.

"Can I get you anything?" Rose asked, just wanting to get away. There were eleven other tables, and most of them were packed full. Lavender had been doing a great job of making sure that this table had been taken care of without Rose having to spend much time at it.

"No. Palmer and Ames were just saying that Derek Fields had moved back into town, and I was wondering if you had heard the news. You and he were in the same class in school, weren't you?"

"We were," Rose said, remembering Derek well. And also having heard bits and pieces of the gossip that had been going on in his life.

"His grandparents weren't doing very well," Charlene said, her face showing her concern.

"I was disappointed to hear that. Their spread isn't far from ours, and I think his grandparents were thinking about selling. Now he's back, hopefully to help them and keep the farm from being sold," Palmer said, leaning casually back in his chair, one arm around his wife, Ames, whose rosy cheeks and athletic build suited someone who worked at the Olympic training center that had been built several years ago just outside of Sweet Water. "Although I suppose I would have been interested in buying."

"I don't think we have time for more land anyway, Palmer," Ames said, smiling at her husband, her eyes twinkling. Like she knew exactly what he was going to say.

"A farmer always has time for more ground," he said, and Ames's smile just got bigger, like that was exactly what she had been expecting.

They didn't get out without their four children too much, but they still acted like a young couple in love, not like they were approaching middle age. They must be in their forties since they had both been older than her in school.

"He might not be interested, but he was when he was younger," Charlene said, and Rose nodded, remembering that Derek had wanted to settle down on his grandparents' farm, but he'd ended up moving to The Cities because the girl he was with didn't want to marry a farmer.

"If you're trying to match Rose up, I know for a fact that Derek and Rose would be terrible together. Derek's been living in The Cities for over ten years, and he's very debonair. He might have grown up here in Sweet Water, but he's not a hick anymore. I've actually spoken to him several times, since our parents are good friends." Leah joined the conversation from across the table, and Rose shifted her body just a little so that she wasn't being completely rude by blocking her out.

Even though she wanted to.

"Rose is quite a catch, and any man would be crazy not to be interested in her," Charlene said, despite the fact that Harry had obviously been not interested in her.

Leah picked up on that right away. "I think that's a false statement. After all, Harry has excellent taste."

"Might be the other way around," Harry muttered, maybe referring to the fact that he thought any man who was interested in Rose would be crazy.

Rose wasn't sure, and she didn't ask for clarification.

Ames and Palmer were whispering at the other end, and Ty and Louise hadn't even looked up from where their heads were bent together. They were taking the whole sweethearts' banquet thing literally. Maybe because they'd spent so much time apart before they'd finally gotten together and gotten married, or maybe that's just the way their relationship was, but they always seemed to be deeply involved with each other. Almost to the point of shutting the world out like they didn't even realize there *was* a world.

Rose wouldn't mind a relationship like that. Where some man wanted her so much that he didn't care about the rest of the world.

He was only interested in her.

It was a nice daydream but probably something that would never happen. She'd have to get past the idea that all men were cheaters.

Even though she knew it wasn't so, she really didn't want to go back down that road. As much as she wanted to be cherished and loved by someone, longed to be, she also did not want to be the laughingstock of everyone ever again in her life.

"It's okay, Rose. After all, we need people to serve the sweethearts' banquet, and you can hardly do that if you're with someone," Harry said, and maybe there was a slight smirk on his face, or maybe that was just Rose's imagination.

"Actually, I am with someone," she said.

She wanted to slap her hand over her mouth. That wasn't the slightest bit true. Why had she said it?

And why wasn't she correcting herself immediately?

But she didn't and allowed herself a bit of a smug look at the astonishment on Harry's and Leah's faces.

Why was she doing this? She was just going to have to confess the truth and be embarrassed.

"Oh? That's interesting," Leah said, rolling her eyes a little, and Rose turned away. Already ashamed of her lie.

Knowing she should just admit that the words had popped out, almost in self-defense, maybe because her heart was just so tired of being painfully beaten up all the time. So it threw those words up and out they came.

Yeah. If only. It just showed a lack of character on her part. That she would prefer to lie rather than graciously accept the truth.

"I heard rumors of you with someone. It's getting pretty serious now?" Charlene said, and Rose managed to not fall on her neck and kiss her, but it was hard.

"It is. He's a great guy. He's so honest. And he doesn't lie." Like those were two separate things. Yeah. She hadn't realized she could be so catty.

"You want a good man with character. Don't settle for anything less," Charlie said from the other side of Charlene. He didn't typically talk much, but when he did, Rose always listened. Usually what he said was wise and laced thoroughly with common sense.

"Yeah. Some of us have learned that the hard way," Rose said, wanting to back away from the table and leave before any of the other couples heard what they were saying and asked her about it. Right now, it was just Leah and Harry, it wouldn't be a big deal.

"What's his name?" Leah asked, of course. Of course she would ask what his name was.

"Would you mind filling up my glass, please?" Charlene said immediately, holding up her mostly full glass of water. "I'm not sure how all the ice melted. I don't like it when it gets to room temperature."

Charlene had specifically requested no ice in her glass when they'd been pouring it earlier.

Grateful for the reprieve, Rose took it immediately. "Of course."

"So there's no name to this mystery boyfriend?" Leah said, like that's exactly what she was expecting.

"Of course not. There is no name, there's no man, and there won't ever be. For reasons that are obvious to everyone," Harry said, and there was no question that he was being a jerk. Rose couldn't even try to find a way to sugarcoat that.

"Oh, there is one all right," Miss Charlene said. "They're all signed up for the Dating Game fun night we're having next month. In fact, they're probably the couple most likely to win." Maybe Miss Charlene's voice was slightly higher than normal, since it seemed to carry over all of their table, and several people at the next table looked over.

As much as Rose wanted to hug Miss Charlene, she also wanted to shake her. How was she going to get out of this lie now? She'd have to have a major breakup with a mystery man she didn't even know the name of.

"Interesting," Leah said, acting like she knew for a fact that everyone around her was lying.

Funny, because they had just been talking about people with character and how honesty was a trait to look for.

Apparently Rose didn't even qualify to date herself.

"I'm definitely looking forward to that. You can sign Harry and me up." Leah smiled at Harry, and they shared a romantic kiss. "I'm sure that true love will win the day, and Harry and I will come out on top," she said, not even trying to be subtle anymore.

Rose held up Miss Charlene's glass. "I'll be back in a minute."

She walked away, wondering how she got herself into these kinds of things.

No. She knew.

She'd spent years and years and years with a lie never crossing her lips, always being honest, always doing right, always choosing the best path, and being kind no matter how unkind people were to her, and then one little slipup, one little white lie, one little defense against people who pounded constantly at her bruised and beaten heart, just once, she did something wrong, and immediately judgment fell.

God? It's really not fair.

She knew by now that there was no point in pointing that out. No matter how true it was, it didn't matter. Life wasn't fair. And someone who was good all their life didn't get credit for that if they chose to lie.

She wanted to keep walking, through the kitchen, out the door, and out into the North Dakota vastness.

To be somewhere, anywhere, other than here.

But they still had the Jell-O salad to serve, and the cake, and she couldn't leave until everything was cleaned up, washed, dried, and put away.

"Are you engaged?" Lavender asked, rushing into the kitchen and going straight for Rose.

At the sink, Patty lifted her head and turned around, her mouth open.

"Yes?" Rose focused on pouring cold water into Charlene's glass. Her word came out as a question, not an answer, but apparently that was enough for Lavender.

"You're engaged!" Lavender squealed. "Why haven't you told anyone?" She grinned. "He asked you on Valentine's Day, didn't he? And...wait!!! Who?!"

"I'm sorry. I know you're excited, and I'm sorry I haven't said anything, but I have to get this water back. We can talk in a little bit."

Normally she would never leave her sister like that, but she had no idea of what to say.

She carried the water back to Charlene's table, and thankfully the entire table was engaged in a rousing discussion of the price of corn, and the weather pattern they'd been in, and everyone had their own prediction for what the weather was going to be this year, so she was able to set the water down and slip away.

She went to the table at the far end, where George and Thelma were sitting with their daughter, Gracie. They were the only ones who had brought a child, and they had been seated at the table with Frank and Jean, the only couple who had brought their dog, Blondie.

Technically, neither kids nor dogs were supposed to be at the banquet, since it was a sweethearts' banquet, but no one made anyone strictly adhere to the rules, and if they couldn't find a sitter or didn't want to leave their dog at home, it wasn't a big deal.

It was Sweet Water after all, and people rolled with things.

So far Gracie and Blondie had been eyeing each other, and it seemed like Gracie wanted to pet the dog, but Blondie didn't seem too interested in children, ignoring people in general.

"Blondie's home all the time so we had to bring her, because she needs to be socialized. We want to get her certified to be an elderly companion, and in order to do that, Blondie needs to be socialized while she's young with lots of people," Jean had explained to Rose when she'd first gone over to serve them, although Rose hadn't asked and certainly didn't care if the dog was at the sweethearts' banquet.

Blondie lay beside Jean, her ears flattening against her head every time Gracie looked at her.

She was young, and if Rose was any judge of dogs, she was terrified as well.

The other people at the table had been fine as well, and the dog had helped guide them into conversations that involved all the dogs everyone had ever owned with one old-timer telling a story about a blue heeler he used to have and how it went out every night and guarded their home, and with the way the man was embellishing the tale, Rose figured by the time he was done the dog would be making supper and doing rounds in the hospital as well.

Obviously, the guy had been fond of his dog.

Seeing that they were ready for the Jell-O salad, she walked back to the kitchen and grabbed a pan along with some new dessert plates.

"You are awful!" Lavender said as she hurried past, food in one hand and two glasses in the other, and Rose wanted nothing more than to tell her that it was all a big farce. Lavender would understand, even agree. And she'd probably keep up the pretense tonight and help her figure out a way to get out of it.

But she didn't want her sister to have to lie for her. Plus, people were finishing up their meals, and they needed to clear the tables, get dessert plates out, and set out the Jell-O salad and the cake.

"I'll tell you all about it later," Rose said, wishing she didn't have to say anything at all.

"Hey! Is that ours? That looks great!" a man said as she walked by his table with the Jell-O salad in one hand and the dessert plates in the other.

Noticing that his table was ready too, she set the Jell-O salad down along with the plates.

It was another ten minutes before she made it back to the back table with the child and the dog.

By that time, Gracie had gotten bored with no food in front of her and was off her chair, glancing at her parents and obviously trying to move around without them noticing.

She'd probably been told to sit still, but her desire to pet the dog overcame her desire to do what her parents wanted her to.

Rose smiled. She remembered being a child and wanting a dog more than anything. A dog of her own, something to cuddle up with at night, something to go places with, and something that loved her no matter what.

She supposed every child probably went through a stage where they wanted a pet.

Maybe after tonight, George and Thelma would consider doing that for Gracie, since she was an only child and probably lonely.

Setting the Jell-O salad down, she grabbed empty plates so she could pass out the dessert plates, and they'd be ready for cake.

Concentrating on her task, she barely registered that someone at the table had just said that German shepherds make better cattle dogs than blue heelers, which caused something close to a heated argument at the table, when growling and barking and a squeal interrupted everything.

Gracie had managed to move away from her chair and over to Blondie. Blondie must have backed away from her until the dog was cowering against the wall.

By the looks of things, Gracie had figured she would be able to catch Blondie and possibly pick her up, although Rose couldn't be sure. Whatever happened, the dog had been frightened enough to snap at the little girl. Gracie squealed while the dog growled and bit her face.

Rose didn't think twice but yelled, waving her arms and running toward the dog.

Her family owned an auction house, and she dealt with animals on a weekly basis. She helped every Wednesday and Saturday at the auction along with her job at the diner.

They'd never run a dog through the auction barn, but in her experience, any animal could be intimidated if a person looked big and scary enough.

It was also her experience that there were times where it was beneficial to try to calm a scared animal down, to soothe them with pretty words and slow movements.

But when an animal was attacking, especially when a child was involved, it was faster and safer to be big and scary, at least until everyone had been moved out of the danger area and into a safe place.

It was just natural instinct for Rose to do what she did, since it's what she would have done at the auction barn. Sure enough, the dog backed up, and she was able to angle herself, coming in from the side and chasing the dog away from the crying little girl.

Figuring that the dog wasn't coming back—she had only snapped because she was scared of the little creature—Rose knelt down.

Gracie's face was bleeding, and Gracie was sobbing and scared, calling for her mom.

The dog's teeth had yanked down on Gracie's cheek, and there would be a scar, surely, but the wounds weren't fatal.

Thelma took one look and started hyperventilating, fanning herself, looking petrified and anxious.

Rose glanced up, one hand holding the little girl's hand, one hand stroking her head.

"Settle," she said sharply, and Thelma's eyes focused on her. "Look," she said, shifting her voice to a soft, calming tone, hoping that Thelma could hear her over Gracie's sobs. "You need to calm down so Gracie sees you're not scared. She'll be brave if you are."

She didn't have children of her own, but she had babysat a lot of kids through high school. Her whole dream in life had been to be a wife and mother. She knew that wasn't what women were expected to do in the modern world, and it wasn't something that she told a lot of people, but when she got married, it was the one thing she wanted: children.

So maybe she didn't know them like a mother might, but she did have a good bit of knowledge, and she knew it to be true. Children had a tendency to mirror the emotions of the adults they were with.

Whether it was her words, or whether it was Thelma finally coming to her senses, Rose didn't know, but she straightened her face, drew in a breath, and knelt down on the other side of her daughter.

George stepped in, and Rose stood up and backed away so they could kneel on either side of their child.

Her heart hurt, because she was sure the parents were upset with themselves and scared.

Looking up, she could see that Frank and Jean had grabbed a hold of Blondie and had her calmed down. It looked like they were taking her out, and Rose figured that was probably for the best.

Everything seemed to be taken care of, so she went to the kitchen, washed her hands, and went back out to do her job. She felt terrible for not just Gracie, but for her parents, and also for Blondie. Hopefully they'd understand that the dog wasn't a terrible dog, just wasn't ready to be handled by small children.

Regardless, she was grateful that the talk for the rest of the evening was about the dog, the attack, and debate on whose fault it was, along with stories people told about being attacked by dogs or witnessing dog attacks, and everyone seemed to forget that Rose had suddenly become engaged. For the evening anyway.

YOU CAN CONTINUE READING by getting *Cowboy Walking Away* HERE[1].

---

1. https://www.amazon.com/Cowboy-Walking-Coming-Western-Romance-ebook/dp/
B09S19DTCY

Made in the USA
Middletown, DE
19 August 2023

36980742R00106